NATIVE STORIERS: A SERIES
OF AMERICAN NARRATIVES

Series Editors
Gerald Vizenor
Diane Glancy

Praise for Gerald Vizenor's previous work:

"*Wordarrows* is a milestone in the campaign to make traditional native culture a relevant part of modern life. It represents one man's attempt to be both meaningful and honest in using his tribal past."—*Antioch Review*

"[Vizenor's] reading is vast and erudite; his use of it eclectic and ingenuous."—*Choice*

"Vizenor's writing releases words. Those usually kept in their places in the dictionary and the dominant way of thought, but which are alive, words still on the building-meaning block and wished to be loosed to roam again. . . . His book is a campground of many voices. A get-together. A literate powwow."—*Great Plains Quarterly*

"The world needs more independent minds of Vizenor's caliber." —Michael Snyder, *Great Plains Quarterly*

"[Vizenor is] the foremost postmodern theorist of Native American literatures and cultures."—*San Francisco Chronicle*

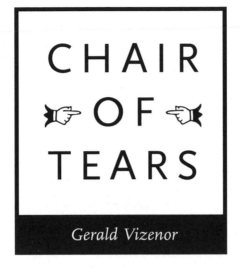

CHAIR
☞ OF ☜
TEARS

Gerald Vizenor

UNIVERSITY OF NEBRASKA PRESS: LINCOLN AND LONDON

© 2012 by Gerald Vizenor
Manufactured in the
United States of America

∞

Library of Congress
Cataloging-in-Publication Data

Vizenor, Gerald Robert, 1934–
Chair of tears / Gerald Vizenor.
p. cm. —(Native storiers: a series of American narratives)
ISBN 978-0-8032-3840-4 (pbk.: alk. paper)
1. Indians of North America—Fiction. 2. Satire. I. Title.
PS3572.19C45 2012
813'.54—dc23
2011033178

Set in Scala by Bob Reitz.
Designed by Ashley Muehlbauer.

In Memory of

John Clement Beaulieu

Karl Kroeber

James Welch

This bird loves to soar among the clouds,
and its cry can be heard when flying above,
beyond the orbit of human vision. . . .

Their innate courtesy and politeness often
carry them so far that they seldom, if ever,
refuse to tell a story when asked by a white
man, respecting their ideas of the creation
and the origin of mankind.

These tales, though made up for the
occasion by the Indian sage, are taken by
his white hearers as their *bona fide* belief,
and, as such, many have been made public
and accepted by the civilized world.

WILLIAM WARREN,
History of the Ojibway People

■ ■ ■

Nature is made to conspire with
spirit to emancipate.

Nature, chapter VI,
RALPH WALDO EMERSON

Contents

☞ 1 ☜

Captain Eighty

Quiver was a natural at feigns and folds, and the unreserved strategies of the game. She never lost a hand of showdown poker in more than fifty years. My clever grandmother won every game by native instinct and chancy moves, not by mere visions or meditation, or a wary mindset, and she surely teased and nurtured children in the same way.

She easily beguiled the newcomers to the reservation—federal agents, teachers, and summer tourists, the steadfast outsiders; and then in her seventies she was invited to teach native students how to feign, fold, pose, and sidetrack the learned professors and players at the university.

Quiver was the native maven of poker scenes.

She married a native storier who roamed in the bush, a curious trickster of discrete grace and mercy. That man, my grandfather, lived by natural reason, by the circles of intimate memories, a native nickname, and always with a necessary sense of the seasons.

He imagined the waves, traces and stories of ancient stones, the shimmer of green dragonflies at sunrise, the great shadows of totemic cranes over the headwaters, the elusive moves of cedar waxwings, high step blue herons in the shallows, the wink and break of leaves in the autumn, the chase of beaver, and the brush of sumac in the snow. He teased me with creation stories of sound, scent, and motion, the wind in the white pine, the scent of moccasin flowers, the intricate weave of spider webs, and the traces of carnal musk on a summer night. The seasons were the natural sources of his sense of presence, reason, and memory.

My grandfather was a storier, and he could envision a bobcat by cautious manner, a trickster raven by avian visions, the necessity of natural flight, the tease of cricket songs at dusk, the heave of black bears in the warm rain, and yet that early spring by more than natural reason and memory, by more than the imagic motion of the seasons, he vowed and then built a marvelous nuptial houseboat on Lake Itasca in Minnesota.

Anishinaabe tricksters are seldom sailors but my grandfather launched that matrimonial houseboat, constructed of timber waste, scraps of milled lumber, rusted oil drums, and a manual makeshift paddle wheel from the blades of a windmill, just outside the treaty boundary to escape the capricious authority of federal agents and sleazy reservation politicians.

Federal agents were the most notorious abusers of natural reason and the ordinary rights of animals and birds. The agents scorned the storiers and visions of hereditary flight, maligned the sovereignty of treaty citizens and the continental liberty of our native ancestors by declarations of civil war, and by the cruel calculations of birth counts, blood rights, and cultural termination. The storiers and sentiments of family traces and the natural currents of our presence were turned to cold blood and racial fractions by federal separatists.

The Anishinaabe have endured by traces of descent.

The Red Lust, decorated with bright plumage, sailed in the summers on Lake Itasca. The hearty crew of children sold carved masks and birch bark scrolls to tourists at the headwaters of the Mississippi River. My grandmother convened poker games on the houseboat at anchor near the resort docks. Eager visitors waited on the shoreline in any weather to board the exotic houseboat for a game of chance with a native gamester.

The houseboat was beached during the winter under the giant red pines near the headwaters. The captain and his crew of mariners and mongrels matured by teases and trickster stories in a wigwam and the heated cabin of the houseboat. The severe winters inspired memorable stories of native survivance. No one could survive the cold and heavy crusted snow without the marvelous moves and adventures of the native trickster in stories.

Spring stories were chancy.

Captain Eighty was a storier of survivance.

Quiver Beaulieu was only sixteen years old at the time of the buoyant spring ceremony, and the trickster storier and captain, my grandfather, was in his seventies. My grandmother told me she was captivated by his tease and stories, and by the nature of his visions, avian visions, because he turned words into names and wings. His stories and rush of resistance to the dummy manners and surnames of the government were enough to demonstrate his passion of survivance, but she was truly enchanted by the music of his native flute. The natural whispers and tremolos of his flue reminded my grandmother of the flute à bec that her father played at night in the boundary waters. The sounds touched the water in a union of music with the loons.

My grandfather played his sumac flute on the night of their native marriage at the headwaters. Naturally, the mighty ravens were radiant and raucous on that maiden voyage of the Red Lust. The mongrels pranced, bounced, bayed, and barked on the deck of the nuptial houseboat.

Captain Eighty smiled for the first time, according to his two dour sisters, when he married my grandmother, and he continued to smile night and day until his death nineteen years later. Truly his smile was as elusive as a bear, wolf, or mongrel. Eighty even grinned in a cold rain, at native wakes, and truly he died with a smile at the rickety helm of the Red Lust. His nickname was derived from the atomic number for mercury.

Quiver and Eighty conceived and nurtured five extraordinary children on a houseboat of native liberty. Three girls, named Two Pairs, Straight, and Full House, and two boys named Flush, and High Card, were teased under paddle and sail on the rough wooden deck and in the cabin of the houseboat. Flush, my father, was the eldest, born two years before the houseboat nuptials, and he was the first to be named for a poker hand.

Poker nicknames were unusual in the course of native names, but our nicknames initiated epochs of memorable stories, and the chance of futurity. My father learned how to read poker hands and how to operate the manual paddle wheel on the houseboat. Every nautical child since then, over two generations, has inherited paddle wheel duty.

Flush married a public health nurse from a nearby reservation hospital. My father had been hospitalized with pneumonia, and was captivated by the round masked face, and the crisp white uniform of the nurse. He told many stories about that mysterious masked nurse at his bedside. The mask muffled her voice, and he did not notice at the time that the nurse of his houseboat dreams was born with one short leg. I mention this condition now, at the start of my ancestral stories about eccentric relatives and their memorable nicknames, because my mother fiercely resisted any nicknames that described her wonky gait, or the signature trace of her right footprint in the snow.

Juliette, my determined mother, declared that she was never a hobbler, and actually denied the native tradition of personal stories and intimate names until she could fully appreciate a favorable ironic nickname. The origin stories of most native nicknames were teases and ironic. My mother never encouraged or conceded to any native nickname, not even to the mundane names Snow Mask or White Foot.

Captain Eighty named my mother Goose Walker.

Quiver praised, teased, and coaxed the children, the mongrels, and most relatives to smile, smile, smile, so it was much easier to believe at the time that she could tame a lusty native of the bush, and a trickster storier, to build a huge houseboat, and to beam at the helm in every season of their marriage.

Quiver was a mighty player.

Eighty was a mighty teaser and testy natural healer. He could shy an animal with a steady gaze, and yet the trickster of mercy rescued and protected abused, maimed, deformed animals, wounded birds, and, of course, many abandoned reservation mongrels. His secure gaze was visionary, a natural scrutiny, and he perceived the seasons of heart, bone, flight, and the curves of nature that precede the words and stories. The mongrels were cautious in his presence, but they moaned, bayed, and barked at his stories.

I was the first nautical grandchild on the houseboat and clearly remember the many mongrels that sailed with my grandfather. Pope Pius, Moby Jean, Monte, Big Wig, Tender, Mustard, and Appetizer were devoted mariners every summer during my early years on the Red Lust. Moby Jean was a huge white mongrel, and she was always close to my grandfather at the helm of the houseboat. Appetizer, a miniature sleeve dog, had been abandoned near a resort at the end of the tourist season. She ran along the shoreline that autumn for three days and barked at the houseboat, and then, once aboard, she circled the deck, nosed the other mongrels, and never barked again. Appetizer was immediately at home on the houseboat, silent and forever loyal to our native nautical family.

Monte, one of my favorite maritime mongrels, had two feathery ginger tails. Truly, two ginger tails, and the tails wagged together in the same direction. Eighty told several stories about how he had rescued the abandoned mongrel with two tails near the headwaters of the Mississippi River. Monte, in fact, swam out to board the houseboat, a mongrel sailor at heart. Since then only three native mongrels have been born with two marvelous ginger tails. Monte, the feathered mongrel, was named for the Monte Cassino Monastery established by Saint Benedict in Italy.

Captain Eighty told me, and every one of his grandchildren, about the Benedictine monks who raised a strain of mongrels with two tails in the fifteenth century at the headwaters of the Mississippi River. These were miraculous trickster stories, and the account of the mongrels with two tails was never the same, but his stories about the wayward monks were consistent.

The Red Lust sailed every summer with these loyal mongrels and wondrous stories. My grandfather incised some of these stories about the monks and the mongrels on birch bark, and we sold these postindian traditional scrolls to tourist at the resorts. Some of his scrolls were acquired by museums as authentic traditions.

I was the firstborn of the grandchildren and heard several variations of the stories about the monks and feathered mongrels. My grandfather never told the same stories because the scenes of stories are visual, not literal. Eighty declared in his stories that the contrary monks had built a monastery about six hundred years ago, raised mongrels with two ginger tails, and at the same time created a manuscript about descriptive erotic pleasures and sexual practices with animals.

Only the best stories create traditions.

The *Manabosho Curiosa* is an arcane manuscript of sensual stories about Benedictine monks, uncertain about their celibacy, and various animals such as rabbits, river otter, beaver, bobcats, skunks, and other creatures of the northern woodland. The most erotic and eccentric stories were about curious sex with snowshoe hares and whitetail deer.

Captain Eighty revealed that the mongrels with two tails were steady sensual partners of the monks. Recent scientific studies have corroborated that the actual parchment of the *Manabosho Curiosa* manuscript, and the particular style of the calligraphy, could have been created in the fifteenth century. I was equally convinced by a research report that ancient pollen from the headwaters was found on the manuscript.

Fleury sur Gichiziibi, the name of the first monastery at the headwaters, and the wayward monks had not survived the wicked winters. An amateur archaeologist found ancient coins, clasps, nails, and other metal objects in native burial sites near the headwaters of the great river. The objects were impressive but have never been confirmed as the actual property of the curious and contrary monks. The stories of the mongrels with two tails are more believable than coins, bits and pieces of metal, about the early presence of monks in the sacred order of Saint Benedict.

Eighty evermore teased the children with trickster creation stories and with his ironic memories of monks and mongrels.

He convinced me that the mongrels with two ginger tails, an original trickster creation, were stolen and exploited as sex slaves by the monks of Saint Benedict. Later, the trickster mongrels, he told me, were once born with two tails, but one tail had receded by the time of the early fur trade. The French fur traders and their lusty songs about the double ginger plumage scared the mongrels to hide their tails for protection, but only one of the tails receded by sentiment, evolution, and, of course, by the speedy nature of trickster stories.

Eighty was an elusive healer by his manner, gaze, and stories. He practiced natural herbal and imagic, mental medicine, and he taught my grandmother how to project a wily wheeze, and with the practice of that deceptive sound of breath, and a slight quiver of a finger, or an eye flutter, she became a natural at showdown poker games.

The Red Lust was our home without a dock.

"Who would not quiver around that nasty old man of the brush?" The federal agent who said that about my grandfather had removed natives from reservation lakeshores and leased the properties to outsiders. Natives were ordered to relocate to remote lonesome federal allotments in the backwoods. That agent was cursed by natives and never fully recovered from a mysterious skin disease, a blotchy sepia pigmentation that he blamed on shamans and in particular my grandfather.

Eighty nicknamed the agent Sepia Face.

Sepia Face, who never disguised his rage, facial rash, welts, streaks, and sepia malady declared that my grandfather could "scare the bark from a birch tree." Sepia Face was a federal freak of nature and native irony.

Eighty was actually a natural at stripping birch bark for baskets and scrolls. He honored the trees, and incised on the soft inner bark many stories about the children on the houseboat, the monks, mongrels with two tails, and he read these pictomythic stories to me, adventure stories about my father, my uncle, and my aunts on the high seas of Lake Itasca.

The winter stories on the houseboat were the most ironic and memorable. Yes, ironic, because severe winters cannot be endured without original tricky stories. The trickster was created over and over again by winter storiers. The best trickster stories are created in extreme winters.

Captain Eighty was truly a natural healer, and he aroused the entire family with his trickster stories. Quiver forever teased the lusty storier and his sense of survivance on the winter houseboat. Naturally, we survived the winters in good health and humor. Our laughter over trickster stories must have heated our bodies and the cabin of the houseboat.

Quiver never truly listened to the federal agents, but she was pleased to tease them to smile and at the same time beat them at poker. Flush, my father, wondered if the agents were determined to lose at poker because they feared my grandfather. Sepia Face and other federal agents and teachers forever lost to my grandmother, and their poker losses supported our marvelous houseboat family.

Quiver envisioned a great armada of houseboats, a native navy of wild poker gamers, a prophetic scheme some fifty years before casinos were launched on treaty reservations. Captain Eighty would moor the armada of poker houseboats that she had envisioned near the headwaters of the Mississippi River.

Meanwhile, my grandmother decided on a lusty storier to bear the dream at the helm of a rickety houseboat with a makeshift paddle wheel and square patchwork sail. She regularly played poker with tourists in the summer, natives and migrants in a fish house on the ice in the winter, and with the most predict-able losers—federal agents, and teachers—on the reservation in any season.

The Red Lust was steady with only a narrow keel, rough hewn and secure, but even so the buoyant houseboat overturned once on the starboard paddle wheel in a severe thunderstorm. Full House, my aunt, drowned in the heavy waves. She was seven years old, a gentle, lanky, quiet child, and the last born on the houseboat. Full House sat next to her mother for more than three years at houseboat and reservation poker games. She learned to read the gestures of the tourists, teachers, and federal agents. The games were her public school tutelage on the reservation, and a worthy cultural education of feigns and folds in showdown poker. Her puffy body washed ashore three days later on August 6, 1945, on the very same day the atomic bomb destroyed the city of Hiroshima, Japan.

Full House directly learned the finger quiver, and other feigns, poses, deceptions, and strategies of poker. Quiver mourned that her daughter would have become a natural at the game, a man-ager of the houseboat casinos. Poker winnings were the primary source of income, the uncertain bluff money of a houseboat family. Quiver inspired everyone to smile, even the losers at poker games, but she never truly smiled again after the death of her daughter.

Quiver created a native touchstone of memory by virtue of chance, by the traces of seasons, ordinary numbers, and by precise dates, although she never used a calendar to constitute a sense of presence. She created and practiced a native sense of presence, memory, and resistance, and by a clever tease of names and stories the sentiments of liberty. Hiroshima, August 6, 1945, for instance, became an epoch signature of our houseboat memories, testaments, survivance stories, and many ironic tributes to native traditions.

Quiver established three marvelous epochs of memory by her tease and stories, but not by the archive documents, histories, or the primers of futurity. The ironic praise and tributes to children on the houseboat were so spontaneous and persuasive day by day that no one could easily move away. Our family was forever bound by teases and stories. Truly the epochs of our houseboat memories were weighty.

The children on the houseboat were educated by natural reason, by the tricky course of the wind and seasons, by stories of native epochs and remembrance. Not one in the family graduated from any federal or mission school. We were a family of mariners. The federal agents considered us marginal and outside the treaties and pale of the reservation, uncounted, a reversal of civilization, and buoyed in obscurity on a creaky houseboat.

Flush was a student at the mission school for seven years, but he could not reconcile the actual lively native sense of presence on the houseboat with that monstrous absence at the priestly heart of monotheism and archive manners. So, at age thirteen, my father declared that he would become a wood carver and a sculptor. He carved native masks from living trees in such a way that the scar on the tree was healed by the ceremonial memory of the mask. Flush first envisioned the masks, and then carved the images by meditation, and a native tradition was created with a precise crack at the very moment the mask was cut free from the tree. The masks were painted with natural pigments to convey the spiritual power of nature and natives. Trickster Healer, one of his early masks, was included many years later in an exhibition at the Musée du Quai Branly in Paris.

Captain Shammer and Dogroy Beaulieu, my closest cousins,

were the only grandchildren who have carried out that sense of presence and survivance in native stories, and the patterns of epoch memory. Shammer, an academic teaser and poseur, was the eldest son of Two Pairs. My cousin earned the ironic nautical nickname of Captain Carbon, and later Captain Six for the atomic number of carbon, because he was so eager to share the helm of the houseboat with our grandfather Captain Eighty.

Dogroy, a distinguished abstract painter, was the son of High Card. Actually, he was an abstract baroque painter who was banished from the reservation because of his exaggerated portrayals of casino gamblers and politicians. There has never been a sense of peace or liberty for painters and literary artists on reservations.

Dogroy painted grotesque images of pale, corpulent gamblers connected to oxygen provided by the casino slot machines. The reservation politicians in a series of portraits were eviscerated and devoured by swarms of maggots. The colors were bright, the slot machines were enormous, and the casino politicians were porky ornaments.

High Card, my uncle, married a feisty native woman on the reservation and assumed her surname Beaulieu, but only as a second nickname. Beaulieu woman had many nicknames, but Grope and Grabble were descriptive and the most familiar. Grope never visited the houseboat because she was reluctant to cross the treaty boundary of the reservation. The federal agents named the condition Removal Agoraphobia.

Captain Eighty never received or assumed a surname, and he refused to acknowledge the summons by federal agents to choose a formal surname for acceptance and treaty reservation certification. The agents might have named his condition Surname Agoraphobia. Clearly he was more appreciated by a nickname, several nicknames, and each familiar moniker created a sense of his native presence, an epoch of memories because the actual native namers were never separated from the tease and stories of the nickname.

Eighty responded only to nicknames in honor of his parents. His father refused to bear the names of outsiders, fur traders, or the federal and mission names of dominance. The family faithfully carried out that natural practice of the native tease and nicknames. Eighty conceded, however, and encouraged his children to assume a formal second nickname, not a surname, but a second intimate nickname. Beaulieu is solely a second nickname, and has never been recorded as a surname in our houseboat family.

Two Pairs and High Card were celebrated and widely known by several nicknames, not only poker hands, and yet they continued the stories of their parents, a native sense of presence in the second nickname of Beaulieu. Straight and Two Pairs insisted that their manly wooers and suitors bear the same fur trade second nickname of the houseboat family.

Captain Carbon Six Shammer are prominent nicknames, and he is the native son of Two Pairs. His nicknames were teases, ironic, imagined, and ceremonial, but never a certified name in an archive. Dogroy was an esteemed nickname of a painter, the son of High Card. His nickname was derived by resonance, not by the evidence of a document. Captain Shammer and Dogroy have the very same second nicknames as simulated surnames, Beaulieu. So, these nickname practices were native epochs of memory.

Quiver was the only child of native fur traders at the end of that great continental adventure in the northern boreal forest. She was nurtured in a canoe on portages in the boundary waters and at summer encampments on Mountain Lake. My grandmother was about two years old when her mother died at seventeen in an epidemic. Peter Beaulieu, her native father, carried on the customs and hearty nostalgia of the fur trade, and always with his daughter at his side. The beaver and other animals were close to extinction at the time. Peter was a hunter by nature and he continued to live by the seasons of scarce animal peltry and wintered at Grand Portage.

My grandmother learned to speak the languages of the fur trade, Anishinaabe, Métis French, and English. Peter Beaulieu had assumed the first and surname of a fur trader, a trade name, only to be recognized at the fur posts. His native nickname was *nagweyaab* or Rainbow. French fur traders were hurried, curious, lusty, and arrogant, and not accustomed to native nicknames. Many natives who were active in the fur trade assumed familiar trade names to be recognized by the English, the French, and the Americans. Naturally, some of these names later became surnames on reservations. Vezina and Beaulieu were surnames and fur trade names. Vezina, the trade name, was badly transcribed by federal agents as Vizenor only on the White Earth Reservation.

Quiver was a reader, not a storier, and she was encouraged by her father to read in French. She read about the culture, romance, and politics of the fur trade, and that literature became a tribute to an epoch of memory. Many, many years later she honored the memory of her father and his associations in the fur trade by reading novels mostly in French. My grandmother praised the novel *La Peste*, or *The Plague*, by Albert Camus, and likened the stories of the plague and medical workers in Oran, Algeria, to the allegories of federal agents, missionaries, and public health emissaries on the reservation. Besides, the unspeakable death of her unnamed mother, an epidemic in the ruins of the fur trade, was the very heart of native stories and literature, the personal and epoch memories of the Métis French.

Quiver read the original *L'étranger*, or *The Stranger*, by Camus, in French, and later in English. She practiced the sounds of every printed word with a Métis accent, and inspired me to read the novel in translation. My grandmother was a newcomer to the critical ideas of literature, and yet she became the very native *biiwide*, or stranger, of the novel by her comments on the philosophies of the absurd and federal nihilism. She told me one summer night on the houseboat, a few weeks after the death of my grandfather, that *L'étranger* was a recurrent sensation of cynical scenes and episodes on reservations.

Captain Eighty reversed the sentiments of literature, he was a mighty storier, not a reader, but even so he might have remarked that *L'étranger* created a severe sense of absence, the utter nihilism of federal agents, and not a native sense of chance, natural reason, survivance, or the mercy of irony. My grandmother encouraged me to read, and literature roused my sense of liberty, but the stories of my grandfather are forever in my memory, more memorable than any book in my library.

Beaulieu is a township named for one of the first native families removed by federal treaty to the White Earth Reservation. Most of these early reservation families were fur trade descendants of that premier union of natives and the emigrant French. François Hudon dit Beaulieu, and Bazile Hudon dit Beaulieu were voyageurs of New France. Bazile married Ogemaugeeshigequay, the daughter of a prominent crane totem orator of the Anishinaabe. Beaulieu, one of the prominent surnames of the fur trade, is an eternal native name, a prominent fur trade name and the second nickname of our houseboat family.

Dogroy Beaulieu was born near the mission church in the

township of Beaulieu. That place on the reservation has become his source of visual stories and artistic creation. Painters and literary artists must imagine a familiar place, a landscape, and that place has become an epoch of memory and a memorial name. Dogroy never studied art, but he alone roused the aesthetic networks of the cosmoprimitive, a new cachet of native art practice and theory, and the notable Cavalier Rouge.

Dogroy was inspired by the painter Marc Chagall and other artists in Der Blaue Reiter, or Blue Rider, an art movement, and initiated the native Red Rider, or Cavalier Rouge, at his famous Gallery of Irony Dogs. Chagall was born in Vitebsk on the Pale of Settlement. Dogroy adopted that sense of political, cultural, and racial restriction and referred to his home and studio in the township Beaulieu as the Pale of the Reservation.

The Beaulieu studio was located on a natural mound near the Wild Rice River, a notorious haven of lonesome and abused women who apparently participated in mutual masturbation. Chance, one of the many Women of the Creature Arts, as they were known at the time on the reservation, lived near the studio and trained mongrels to sense the absence of irony. Yes, the absence, not the presence, of irony. Natives have endured with a sense of natural reason, stories of survivance, and memorable irony. The absence of native irony was a trace of federal corruption and cultural separation. Many agents and some natives had reasons to fear the persistent bark of the irony dogs. Chance could train a mongrel in only a few months to dance and bark in the presence of people who have no sense of irony.

The irony mongrels sense pretense and anxiety.

Chance was born in the presence of marvelous mongrels. Her first memories and stories were about the perception, acuity, and loyalty of incredible reservation mongrels. Some mongrels were shamanic and could sense human diseases, the wicked presence of the *wiindigoo*, and other monsters that teased and tormented the spirit of natives.

Chance, abandoned at four by her mother to taunt and misery, lived with a strange healer and his wild mongrels. Animosh, a wry and ironic nickname that means "dog" in Anishinaabe, trained mongrels to sense diseases of the spirit and body. Animosh tutored his nosey shamanic mongrels at the entrance to the public health hospital on the reservation. Naturally, the nurses dismissed his lusty stories and mongrel practices as a nuisance, a throwback to the ways of wicked shamans. The doctors, however, considered the sense and perception of the mongrels as primary diagnoses of certain diseases, such as diabetes, cancers, unnatural fright, and dreams of monsters. The mongrels barked, bayed, licked, and nosed the sick and worried at the entrance to the hospital.

Chance trained mongrels to bay over deadly sincerity.

Norway, Austria, Singapore, Vatican City, Utah, and North Dakota, were a few of the states with serious deprivations of irony. Chance would not allow anyone to use and abuse the irony dogs in these states. The dogs would have barked day and night over the obvious absence of irony. She warned, however, that many untrained mongrels were constant barkers and that clearly conveys a serious irony deficiency. Recently, she named the sentimental crèche, most global corporations, municipal, state, and federal institutions and agencies, cemeteries, gated communities, cultural fêtes, social service centers, and pride of place parades, as extreme situations for the ordinary expression and detection of unintended irony.

Fêtes and feigns entice the irony mongrels.

The irony mongrels were certified once they danced and barked in specific situations. The mongrels were trained to dance in the presence of civil servants and bureaucrats, priests and big belly politicians and bean counters, and then to bark at the sentimental intonation of poems in Hallmark Cards.

Lévi-Strauss, Turnip, Nixon, and several other irony dogs were naturals at the detection of congruous postures, virtuosos of the absence of irony games. Lévi-Strauss, for some obscure reason, barked and licked peep toe shoes. Chance explained that some irony dogs could easily sense the absence of irony long before humans perceived the manner. Lévi-Strauss was one of those mongrels with a singular sense of coincidental irony, an unintended ironic harmony. Lévi-Strauss clearly barked and bayed to announce these distinctions and patterns of fortuitous irony, and, of course, the manifest absence of cultural irony.

The graduation ceremony for the irony dog was a walk and bark on a short leash past government centers and federal build-ings to detect the most obvious absence of irony. Lévi-Strauss and the other irony dogs in advanced graduate training were paraded past the simulated scent and sight of the White House, Pentagon, United Nations, Bureau of Indian Affairs, Internal Revenue Service, and the United States Department of State, a virtual Supreme Court of the Absence of Irony.

Lévi-Strauss and one or two other advanced irony mongrels could in most instances sense the distinction between the un-intended irony of Henry Kissinger, Aleksandr Solzhenitsyn, recipients of the Presidential Medal of Freedom, or the *New York Times*, and the notable absence of irony in serious comments by Sigmund Freud, the famous aviator Charles Lindbergh, and Joseph Alois Ratzinger—or Pope Benedict, a citizen of the Vatican.

Chance entrusted me with one of the later mongrel graduates of the irony school. Derrida, one of the most perceptive irony mongrels, was named in honor of the philosopher Jacques Derrida of France. He was a rangy white mongrel with four black paws. Derrida bayed once a week at the Lawrence Welk Show, a musical variety show on television, and later at the tired, tremulous radio voice of Garrison Keillor, the Lawrence Welk of regional peachy poetry and primal scion of Lake Wobegon. The absence of irony was the obvious absence of natives in his curious, clean, and wholesome fictional town of proud and virtuous Caucasians.

Derrida craved the taste of croissants, and, with a similar idée fixe as Lévi-Strauss, the sight of peep toe shoes. Derrida was an outstanding pointer of the native tease, a detector of both the absence and chance of irony. He barked at the latest fashions, hot pants, cat suits, and Afghan coats with fur trim. Derrida was related by sight to the Sloughi from Algeria, and by scent to a Springer Spaniel family from Grand Marais on Lake Superior in Minnesota. He bayed at movie directors, barked at reference librarians, and growled near some of the faculty players at poker games.

Derrida was loyal, always at my side without a leash, and surely he could recite a sonnet in two languages for a buttery croissant in the morning. Parisian tastes and manners, to be sure, but his favorite restaurant was the Band Box Diner near Elliot Park in Minneapolis. Derrida was more secure at the university, not an uncommon manner of irony mongrels, than when he was on the reservation or on busy streets. He clearly associated more with conversations about natural reason, literary art, the dissimilarity of irony, and philosophy. He seemed to listen more closely to lectures than most of the students, especially at aporia seminars on Michel Foucault, Edmond Husserl, and Albert Camus.

Derrida bayed at contradictions and seemed to mourn the absence of aporia. The university faculty was more conservative, empirical, and phenomenological than liberal, structural, or theoretical, and suspicious of academic tourists and irony mongrels; but the most original and confident storiers on the faculty fully embraced the mongrels of irony at seminars and classroom lectures.

Derrida was the pied noir of the seminars.

Dogroy announced that the tradition fascists banished him from the reservation because of the irony mongrels, because the fascists despised his baroque portrayals of corpulent casino gamblers, because he created shrouds of dead animals and birds, and, no less, because of the sexual pleasures he shared with the Women of the Creature Arts. Actually, the tradition fascists were repressive and envious of the native artist who was surrounded by so many curious and creative women. Mostly the tradition fascists resented the singular pleasures of masturbation, and declared that the practice was unnatural, a defilement of native traditions, and the manifest decadence of modern art and civilization. The tradition fascists refused to believe that bears masturbate.

Dogroy was the first native ever banished from a reservation for his shrouds and baroque portrayals. He moved to the city with the irony mongrels and the Women of the Creature Arts. His new studio was located in the former First Church of Christ Scientists in Minneapolis. Dogroy changed the name of the church to the Gallery of Irony Dogs. The banishment was reported widely in the media, and some reporters actually celebrated his right of artistic irony, the right to create animal shrouds and baroque portrayals of casino gamers. The politics of exile actually enhanced his fame as a native artist.

Captain Shammer, my other famous cousin, was appointed by default, and without the customary academic review, the chairman of the Department of Native American Indian Studies at the University of Minnesota. The six previous academic chairmen, each a distinguished native scholar, had failed at departmental governance. The dean, as a measure of desperation and unintended irony, at last hired the absolutely least qualified of the final academic candidates. The notion that the ordinary, the most unremarkable, and the least entitled candidate for the position, could not be worse than the previous six experienced scholars. The radical reversal of academic standards was not exactly a university or native practice, but, in a situation of academic desperation, an ironic senior appointment was considered at the time to be a worthy chance.

Captain Shammer, in about six months' time, became the most original, inspired, admired, and productive chairman in the history of the department. He clearly demonstrated his capacity to manage the faculty, and to inspire entrepreneurial associations, with only the slightest academic qualifications. My cousin avoided an institutional education and never graduated from any school, a tradition of the houseboat descendants. That absence of academic credentials and eligibility, however, became a preposterous appointment and ironic entitlement. Credentials were never used against him because my cousin created a sensational prominence and sense of presence by stories of survivance, not shame, and never by the sentiments of victimry in the governance of the department.

Quiver was generous but at the same time suspicious of the chance and ironic triumph of her grandiose grandson, the eager carbon captain of the family houseboat. Only in a native trickster story would my cousin be named an academic administrator. My grandmother teased the untaught university professor all the more for his chancy appointment as the lucky seventh chairman of the department. That summer, however, he was never more than the second captain, forever the second, of the Red Lust.

☞ 2 ☜

Chair of Tears

Captain Shammer was nominated early that summer by the eccentric and humane Dean Colin Defender to become the seventh and final chairman of the troubled and tormented Department of Native American Indian Studies.

Shammer was bemused by the nomination.

My cousin had never applied, auditioned, or petitioned for the position, and he never had any contact with the previous chairmen of the department. Moreover he had never attended a university or graduated from any school, and had never served in the military, certainly not as an officer, but he arrived promptly at the first faculty meeting of the academic year smartly costumed in the duplicate uniform—tunic, epaulettes, brass buttons, white gloves, and with a regulation cavalry sword—of the notorious and foolhardy General George Armstrong Custer.

Shammer posed at the threshold of the spacious conference room, saluted the faculty, and then, at parade rest, he waited for the inevitable countercries of vengeance, but the faculty, mostly former chairmen, and several graduate students, were stupefied, overcome by the ironic military resurrection, and instead the faculty hailed the general with cavalry hoots, howls, and horsey laughter.

Captain Shammer had arrived by mimicry.

Several faculty members thought the farcical general and poseur professor of mockery might actually succeed by pretence as the seventh chairman of the department. The manner of trickery, ostentation, mockery, and outrageous entrepreneurial notions and measures of governance had never been a dedicated practice in native studies. Each of the six previous chairmen had failed at governance in ordinary academic conventions and casual attire, wrinkled shirts, loose neckties, corduroy sport coats, and, of course, with the most admired high status doctorates. The faculty had no personal military adventures or extreme cuts of consciousness, and no one had ever pretended to be a dead general from the Battle of the Little Bighorn. The six past chairmen had been honored and decorated as learned, rational, theory haughty academics, and yet they flunked as innovative native executives. They had deserted storiers, practices of natural reason, and survivance, and disregarded the very emotive sentiments of a native presence.

Captain Shammer teased the academic conventions.

Sham, shame, shamel, shamus, shammer, shaman, are natural teases and processions of his nickname, but never a doctor, never a professor or general. Shammer had earned the tease and doctored honors of his native nickname from our grandfather at the creaky helm of the Red Lust.

The faculty search committee was overwrought and exhausted by the recurrence of the nasty academic politics that surrounded the previous failed native chairmen. The literature reviews, interviews, dubious praise and hurried celebration of new candidates, and the tiresome exercise of academic hires, persuaded the search committee to nominate an outsider, a native newcomer and innate scholar of natural reason from the headwaters as the seventh chairman of the department. The decision was made by chagrin, reversion, default modes, and by the remarkable chance of irony.

Captain Shammer was assuredly an outsider, and with dubious distinction. He was a master of mockery, and with a humane sense of native presence. The faculty had never heard of my cousin. His presence, not his absence, was more memorable. One student on the search committee recognized his name, and his nautical family. She was from the White Earth Reservation.

The other three final candidates for the position were highly qualified, and each one presented an impressive record of native academic achievements, service, and publications. The search committee reasoned by catchy analogies and obvious contradiction, however, that the six previous eminent appointments had backfired, degenerated by conspiracy, and then one after another collapsed as the chairman of the department.

My cousin was clearly the least credentialed, and yet by far the most interesting candidate because he had not actually applied for the position. His curriculum vitae, constructed by a student, listed only his designation as a captain of a houseboat. That designation of captain was apparently mistakenly handwritten as "chaptain." One committee member was convinced that the candidate was an ordained military minister, the modest native chaplain of a naval houseboat.

Shammer was the carbon captain of the Red Lust.

Chaplain Shammer arrived for his first meeting with Dean

Colin Defender carrying a miniature birch tree under his arm, a gesture of natural reason and contradiction. The birch distraction was strategic. The tree was green, alive, and naturally generated analogies and stories about the dead birch tree in the department, and the traditional incised birch bark scrolls of the Anishinaabe. The dean was genuinely curious about any native traditions.

John Neihardt once concocted the untrue notion that the sacred native tree was dead, my cousin told the dean, and the sacred circle broken at the very end of the popular biblical translation of *Black Elk Speaks*. Neihardt was a poet and honored by natives. He might have been persuaded by the publisher to conclude the visionary stories with a dead sacred tree, invariably a native absence and tragedy, the most familiar themes of commercial literature about natives. The dead tree is a sign of victimry, not a sense of native resistance or survivance.

Shammer noticed earlier that the birch tree in the department had been dead for more than five years, and had never been nurtured in the course of the six washout chairmen. The broken branches were decorated with golden tinsel and bright party ribbons as a holiday disguise. My cousin reckoned that the arcane strategy of a nurtured birch tree was persuasive and memorable. Surely the dean would remember the living tree, the stories of survivance over tragedy and victimry, and connect these images later in the semester.

Dean Colin Defender presumed the miniature birch was a native ceremonial, and so he honored the potted tree with obscure hand gestures. Slash and Burn, as he was fondly known at the faculty club, bluntly asked the trickster what would be his very first decision as the chairman of the department. Shammer solemnly set the living birch tree in the center of the conference table, touched the thin leaves, turned silently and stared at the dean, and then declared that he would post at once the entire department for sale to the most intriguing bidder at a widely advertised public auction.

Chaplain Shammer could not have made a wiser declaration under the circumstances of his incredible appointment as chairman of the remains of a department. Slash and Burn was impressed by the audacious and original response of my cousin. The dean appreciated his decisive untutored entrepreneurial manner, and his conception of academic management and futurity.

The mistaken chaplain was formally named the chairman the very next morning. The search committee argued that credentials, doctorates, and published monographs were immaterial in the same sense that there were no natural bona fides, documents, or native evidence to authenticate a shaman or visionary, a memorable storier, a professor, governor, senator, guardian of the miniature birch or even the president of the United States.

Chaplain Shammer, according to the hasty university press release about his remarkable appointment, had served his country honorably as a distinguished chaplain on a military houseboat and cruiser in the United States Navy.

The Department of Native American Indian Studies had died more times in the past decade than the actual crash and rotation of the six chairmen. The birch tree had expired, and the department was barren, without a vision, a survivance story, or a native sense of irony. Daily the native parties of tedious heritage poachers and whingy militants huffed and puffed in new cowboy hats and boots, plastic bone chokers, and fringed leather jackets about the desecration of native traditions by academic white men. At least once a semester a wave of students called for the tradition fascists to teach the truth about native cultures on reservations.

The student waves were a pretense for easy final grades. Truly, no one wanted to hear more twitchy lectures about the truth of native cultures, and certainly not by tradition fascists from venal casino reservations. Anyway most of the older student protesters were at the university for the generous academic subsidies and had never completed a rigorous university course for credit.

One faculty faction argued for more established, professional native scholars, the published academic celebrities, as it were, to impress other academic departments and to persuade the regents to increase the budget for native studies. The other faction demanded that the university appoint a new chairman with real experience in native communities. The romancers, militants, students, fascists, and tradition mockers were rarely motivated by native history or literary art. The teasers, poseurs, onanists, commune hucksters, and, of course, the most eminent native professors failed entirely, and in every respect, to advance natural reason, transform the course of native studies, or even to save the miniature birch tree in the department. The sacred birch tree died in the presence of ersatz traditions and ideologues. The past native chairmen had no sense of the politics, sentiments, or critical cues of academic survivance.

The sacred tree was dead, dead, dead.

Slash and Burn, true to his nickname, announced a radical, punitive reduction of the annual university funds provided to the Department of Native American Indian Studies. The anxiety was feigned because salaries were excluded from the budget reductions, but the faculty and students were obligated to raise special program money, for the first time, from outside the security of the university, from corporations, foundations, and from ordinary donors in the community.

The showdown militants and crown culturists were enraged,

as always, and they demanded high dudgeon reparations for stolen native land and desecration of traditions. The newspapers reported on native victimry but seldom on native survivance, and the readers were reunited by everyday mea culpas, a daily ritual of cultural forbearance and dominance.

Meantime, the faculty was divided into six rather mundane factions associated with the past chairmen, a convenient political division of native academics and separatists, and the students were distracted by the promises of overnight reparations. Native literary artists, painters, historians, dancers, composers, and medical doctors were never mentioned in the politics of atonement and victimry.

The Black Hills was an eternal visionary presence.

Slash and Burn was dedicated to the commercial development of the department, a new academic enterprise with private motives, entrepreneurial manners, fiscal strategies, and global economics, a continuation of the already slippery commerce in cultural and practical courses at universities. The dean was clearly obliged by the controversial appointment of the seventh chairman, in as many years, to name the academic position the Chair of Tears in the Department of Wounded Hearts.

Captain Shammer was the first person to consecrate or occupy the dubious Chair of Tears. My cousin arrived by chance, and at the precise moment to promote the ironic stature of the department at a public auction. The Chair of Tears was a suitable but uncertain endowment, secured with unintended survivance irony. The tears of the chair, always an ambiguous metaphor, were associated with the breakdown of the past six chairmen, but never teary enough to save the departmental birch tree. The position was more torment than tears, more misery than tease, a political guise of some extraordinary academic and political rendition. The senior faculty was regularly driven to the simulation of tears, at least the feign and fakery of tears, by the extreme declarations, actions, auctions, and primal edicts of the seventh chairman. Marion Boas Fox named my cousin, and with intended irony, Our Beloved Chairman Chaplain. Boas Fox was a prominent accessory linguist and tracery anthropologist in the department. She had earned her doctorate in Heavy Ethnic Notions of Consciousness at the University of California, Santa Cruz.

The Chair of Tears was more irony than victimry.

The number of faculty, students, and visitors increased at each faculty meeting in anticipation of the theatrical appearance of the trickster chairman, Our Beloved Chairman Chaplain. Shammer in the next three months wore masks, bright hats, samurai surcoats, and academic robes at faculty meetings.

The first masks were wooden images, shamanic visions, and some with twisted faces. Flush, my father, carved the masks from living trees near the headwaters. Shammer wore other synthetic masks that resembled famous authors, native leaders, and politicians. His favorite masks were White Cloud, the eminent native mediator of the Anishinaabe, Chief Joseph, the spiritual diplomat, the white hair, nasty gaze, and heavy frowns of Elizabeth Cook Lynn, the tender mercies of Simon Ortiz, the lovely countenance of LaDonna Harris, Jesus Christ in a turkey feather bonnet, three presidents, Theodore Roosevelt, Harry Truman, and Richard Nixon, and the mask of the movie actor, John Wayne.

Captain Shammer wore the White Cloud mask in the company of federal agents, university attorneys, and regents, the Cook Lynn mask of weighty frowns to intimidate the native nationalists and militants, and the Jesus mask in seminars and faculty meetings, the crossblood shaman and trickster who turned nasty metaphors into common praise. Shammer teased the students that he could walk on water in the Jesus mask. He wore the Ortiz mask of ironic mercies at fern bars and poetry readings, the rosy mask of Harris at political protests, and the solemn Chief Joseph mask in the company of native healer dealers at over the barrel summits. My cousin wore the presidential masks and presented carved peace medals at the auction of the department and at various academic conferences.

The John Wayne mask was not comparable.

Sedona, Arizona, that miraculous center of ostentatious healers, spirit dealers, simulators of cures, hot and cold, and antidotes to fear, caprice, and interior voices, was the natural site of the first auction of the department, lock, stock, and barrel to the highest bidder.

Charlatan shamans, and the real politics of parvenu money, sidetracked the wealthy romantic bidders, and the rich, buck fever divorcées and widows who were moved by the stories of native nicknames and victimry. The many chancy connivers, native mind menders, and spirit healer dealers diverted my cousin from the serious auction of the department. Shammer actually revoked the auction in favor of a weekend of nudity, colonic irrigation, and native trickster stories in the mother sauna at the Pink Buffalo Resort.

The Edicts of Shammer were hurried and headstrong that first semester in the department. The faculty was troubled by the mere mention of change, but the students were encouraged by the radical schemes and edicts of the day.

Captain Shammer announced at a press conference in his first month as chairman that the native students were invited to the Patchy Honoring Ceremony. That evening he boldly declared that incomplete grades would be changed to passing grades on student transcripts. Naturally the university registrar was incredulous that any chairman would proclaim an arbitrary change of incomplete grades. Native students had earned incomplete grades in more than seventy percent of registered courses in the past several years.

The Patchy Honoring Ceremony converted more than three thousand credit hours from a record of incomplete to a passing grade. The grade change edict actually encouraged many native students to return to the university and continue their studies in the department.

Finally, near the end of the first semester as chaplain of the Chair of Tears, after he had revoked a spurious treaty and removed the faculty from their private offices, he started to wear masks that resembled the senior faculty. The trickster chairman wore the faculty masks around the campus, and sometimes he changed faculty masks over lunch at the faculty club. The resemblance was obvious, the students were amused, and the faculty was bemused, but clearly there was more political intrigue, pleasure, and persuasion in the gesture of masks than otherwise.

The faculty renounced their own masks.

Captain Shammer teased the faculty to create a mask, or wear the masks of their own character, but they refused to participate in the gesture and irony of images, or even in the native chance of mythical and totemic associations.

Sometimes my cousin wore the masks of his enemies, a clever and imagic manner of resistance, and, of course, ironic survivance. Shammer was convinced that the past chairmen would have been more at ease in masks of their own faces. The faculty might have told the truth in a mask, but instead they marched over the bridge to lunch at the faculty club with blunt faces and tragic memories of a dead birch tree.

3

Removal Treaty

Captain Shammer initiated and ordained more than thirty edicts, radical schemes and teases, political roundabouts, and academic conversations to restructure the department in the first semester of his reign as the trickster chairman. Early that autumn, for instance, on a cold and windy morning, my cousin held a traditional native wake and burial ceremony with hand drums and native songs near the river to honor the dead birch tree, and, at the same time, he terminated the faculty treaty rights to occupy private offices in the department.

Shammer declared at the ceremony that he would never allow anyone to endanger the spirit of another birch tree in the department. The faculty was casual and unconcerned about the mortality of the birch tree, and the students could not even remember when the sacred tree had withered and died in the main office. Sadly, that was not an unusual circumstance because the faculty could not remember when the river frothed at the mouth, choked on the rapids, and died of pollution near the university. So, my cousin would never trust the faculty with the vision, natural reason, and stories of trees, birds, bears, and rivers.

Slash and Burn was scarcely sensitive to animals, plants, birds, or rivers, but he was a natural at academic politics. He decided to secure, protect the potted miniature birch tree mounted on a copper pedestal in the outer office. He instructed his secretary to dutifully water the birch twice a week.

Naturally, the media covered the riverside ceremony for the dead birch tree and the new chairman. Slash and Burn, at the same time, released a feature story about the significance of the sacred tree in his office, and reverently proclaimed October 22, 1964, as the authentic death date of the Mississippi River near the University of Minnesota. Jean-Paul Sartre, the existential philosopher and novelist, declined the Nobel Prize for Literature on that very same day in France. That date became one more epoch of houseboat memories.

Captain Shammer delivered the formal academic initiatives, edicts, pronouncements, and declarations every week of that first semester on birch bark scrolls. He was a modern *voyageur*, a forthright storier in the remembrance of the fur trader, and he was a strategic advocate of native emblems, nicknames, and the many traces of ironic traditions.

My cousin was not a romancer. Rather, he was a teaser of manners, missions, and conventions, and clearly more sensitive to chance and situational conscience than to customary academic practices. So, by the course of natural reason and native stories of survivance his cosmoprimitive visions and postindian revisions became the source a new academic fur trade, swift, decisive, and resolute.

Captain Shammer was a premier native teaser, and always

evasive at the helm of the houseboat and the department. He was a master of contradiction, the high points of irony, and he mimicked the dead languages of academic governance. Indian Studies has no past, he declared at the faculty club, and future studies had no future tense. The native tease was intuitive, derived from natural reason, to be sure, but the intense manner of the tease, the practice of bait and ridicule, was more about unreserved resistance, personal insecurities, and coincidence than about a sixth sense. Yet, by natural reason, strategic mime, mentor mockery, tricky concessions, and ironic praise of the faculty, he clearly perceived the situation as unwitting postindian decadence, a cultural malaise and breakdown of the department.

The native tease, masks, mockery, and situational ridicule were the crucial maneuvers of cultural and academic transformation. The faculty had earned doctorates, honorary degrees, published obscure essays and monographs, and assumed many, many entitlements, by means of institutional tenure and a fantastic academic treaty. My cousin, the trickster and carbon captain of a rickety houseboat, terminated the notion of private offices as a provision of faculty tenure and a spurious treaty.

Captain Shammer asked me to contact native artists to design the original calligraphy of the edicts and decrees that were inscribed on birch bark scrolls. Naturally, we turned to the inventive talents of our houseboat family. Dogroy, my cousin and exiled artist, was enthusiastic about the new edict scrolls, and created several baroque images and script in the style of the original pictomyths incised on the traditional birch bark scrolls by the early Anishinaabe. The scrolls were bound with wide red ribbons, and the ribbons were decorated with native totemic seals created by cosmoprimitive art students of the Cavalier Rouge.

Shammer was determined to enlist and oblige the entire native community in the transformation of the department. He practiced natural reason, shared stories of trickster governance, and mocked the academic pretensions of tenure and the expectation of treaty rights to private offices.

The William Warren Memorial Library, once the most impressive special collection of native books, academic journals, newspapers, documentary movies, microfiche, photographs, and video equipment in the world, steadily eroded with the wane and dissolution of the past six chairmen until there was nothing left on the shelves but empty journal boxes and five unsalable books: *Hanta Yo: An American Saga* by Ruth Beebe Hill; predictably an unread copy of *Indi'n Humor: Bicultural Play in Native America* by Kenneth Lincoln; a broken copy of *The Primal Mind: Vision and Reality in Indian America* by Jamake Highwater; a coffee-stained copy of *Earthdivers* by Gerald Vizenor; and an appropriately defaced copy of *The Education of Little Tree* by Forrest Carter, also known as Asa Carter, who wrote the supremacist political sermon "segregation now, segregation tomorrow, segregation forever" for George Wallace, the late racist governor of Alabama. That abominable sermon on race was scored in capital letters on the cover of *The Education of Little Tree*.

The criminal erosion of a native library.

Yes, erosion, that was the very word the previous academic dean repeated in his official report to describe the outright thievery. The native faculty and students borrowed the books and journals forever, by some obscure sense of entitlement and right of discovery, and outsiders swiped what remained of the memorial library. The strangers were not students or readers, to be sure, but rather they were book and movie rustlers for fast money.

The library was named for the first Anishinaabe historian and member of the territorial government. The Minnesota Historical

Society published the *History of the Ojibway People* by William Warren in 1855, more than a decade before the federal treaty that established the White Earth Reservation, and more than a century before the University of Minnesota set in motion the Department of Native American Indian Studies.

The *History of the Ojibway People* was apparently the most popular book in the department. Thirteen copies were stolen from the library in the past three or four years. Nine copies of the early *Dictionary of the Ojibway Language* by Frederic Baraga were stolen in the same period of time. Three copies of *House Made of Dawn* by N. Scott Momaday went missing in the past year. Each new chairman ordered several more copies of the *History of the Ojibway People* and the *Dictionary of the Ojibway Language* ostensibly for the thieves of native library books. The erosion of the special collection library was an erosion of irony, and a native sense of presence and survivance. The thieves were mundane, mercenaries of dominance, not the native celebrants of oral stories or native literature. The books were stolen to trade and hawk, not to read.

Slash and Burn must have been uncertain and cautious about some of the radical edicts and parodies, but he never countered the new chairman, and never misused or abused the formal documents of incised calligraphy and images on the birch bark scrolls. The dean told a newspaper reporter, "Captain Shammer has brought new blood to the department, and his many edicts have saved and conserved money at a time of a serious fiscal crisis at the university." Slash and Burn promptly apologized for the unwise use of the words "new blood" in his comments. The notion of new native blood insinuated the metaphors of elder blood, dead in the water blood, or better blood, the blood and romance of the fur trade, bloody colonial conquests, the bloody keynotes of civilization, the heavy blood of nationalism, and the get away blood of postindian modernism. So much depends on the bloody cues, praise, myths, and metaphors of ancestry and native memory.

New blood, old blood, native blood, savage blood, half-blood, mixed blood, cross-blood, white blood, red blood, black blood, blond blood, first blood, cold blood, thin blood, young blood, cut and run blood, give blood, take blood, and declare the obvious that blood is thicker than water, a bloody truth game, but never, never trust the blood of federal agents.

Captain Shammer ran on the blood and memories of the fur trade, but the faculty was not sympathetic about the count of beaver pelts or the fancy dance of the *voyageur* and *coureur de bois* on a marvelous portage.

Slash and Burn was much more enthusiastic in private about the native edicts, but he was never critical of my cousin or the edicts and singular administration of the department. At times he carried birch bark scrolls to lunch at the faculty club and read the inscribed edicts to his colleagues at the high table. No one would have suspected that the dean was romantic about natives, and yet he collected and preserved each of the original document birch bark edict scrolls in a special case, located near the miniature birch bark tree, and many years later he contributed that valuable collection of native edict art to the Minnesota Historical Society.

Captain Shammer delivered the treaty termination notice that removed the faculty from private offices to the conference room one early morning in late autumn. The fragile color of the leaves shivered in the bright sunlight and reflected on the dead river. The faculty was anxious, a common trait on the entire campus, slow and moody, gloomy, a rather solemn procession of native scholars in the throes of an authentic academic removal, but the obvious declarations of resistance were only tentative.

Madeline Seams, graduate student, teacher, and a doctoral candidate in native philosophies, was not pleased with the responses of the senior faculty. The old faculty, she declared, was egocentric and mean spirited to protest the participation in a communal native space. Seams reproached the faculty, but her manner was more monotheistic than native and failed to arouse any sense of obligation or conscience. She then pleaded that the faculty had only been removed from the false privilege of a private place provided by the state government. Seams tried to put the faculty to shame, that they had never been removed from any native communities by federal agents, or the cavalry, and had never been forced to march in extreme circumstance to Indian Territory, Bosque Redondo, or hunted down by soldiers at Sand Creek or Wounded Knee. The senior faculty only had to survive the windy winter walk across a covered bridge to lunch at the faculty club.

Four younger faculty members mumbled that the chairman was a mere animal, a wolverine, and in particular a capricious federal agent, but at the same time they packed books and documents and prepared for removal from their private offices.

Clarke Chambers, a historian from another department, was inspired by the communal edict and immediately vacated his adopted office. The older and senior faculty of the department, including the six degenerate chairmen, more secure and lackluster by tenure, cursed and shouted obscenities, houseboat fascist, headwaters dunce, and other nasty bloodline slander at the current chairman.

Captain Shammer was cursed even more as he changed masks from White Cloud to Elizabeth Cook Lynn, and later to John

Wayne. One by one, later in the day, the senior faculty locked their private offices, posted arcane messages about native treaty rights and sovereignty on the doors, protested the authority of the chairman, and refused to teach their courses or move to the common conference room in the department.

Chambers, professor of social welfare history, was the first faculty member to celebrate the radical termination of private offices, and he was the first to move to the conference room. Clarke told the graduate students that the communal edict was an unusual revival of the early neighborhood settlement houses, a sentiment of community. He recounted the dedication of Jane Addams at Hull House in Chicago.

Seams, inspired by the stories of settlement houses, enlisted the support of the graduate students to name the communal conference room the Chambers House. Clarke was so honored because he was the first faculty member to celebrate the natural return to communal academic experience and maturity.

The faculty clearly had no tenure or treaty rights to private offices, an unnatural sentiment of absence and separation. Privacy was a denial of a native sense of presence. Private offices stimulated an elusive sense of nostalgia and melancholy.

My cousin presumed the faculty should have inherited an essential sense of responsibility and cultural duty to practice and encourage at least a trace of native communal traditions, conventions, shareable academic memories, and survivance stories. The birch bark edict of removal proclaimed that the faculty was obligated to move and create a commons, a native sense of presence, an actual active communal presence, not a native absence, and to share the space of the departmental conference room, one huge office for the entire faculty.

Privacy was a sentiment of separatism.

The former faculty offices were designated as the exclusive centers of native communal activities, clearly a natural native conversion and radical transformation of separatism, conspiracies, fantasies of privacy, and nostalgia. The offices were converted to distinctive sites of native visions, resistance, trickster consciousness, natural reason, feigns of fortune, panic, irony, last lectures, traces of cosmoprimitive art, and the stories and practices of survivance.

Captain Shammer named and entrusted the vacant library and seven private offices as singular sites of various native pursuits and creative ventures. The Full House Casino, for instance, was situated in the William Warren Memorial Library. The seven private offices were named for specific visions and distinctive native actions and practices. The obscure native practices located in the seven converted faculty offices were named the Panic Hole Chancery, Irony Dogs, Skin Dunk, Last Lecture, Postindian Holograms, Denivance Press, and Stray Visions.

☞ 4 ☜

Full House Casino

Quiver married a lusty trickster, a marvelous storier of natural reason, and with a native sense of presence, survivance, and generous irony. My grandfather was a woodland dowser of worried hearts, a canny master of favors, and the consummate captain of that nuptial and residential houseboat for nineteen years.

Captain Eighty traded and sold birch bark scrolls, hired out as a guide for tourists and as fishermen in the summer, but he never earned a steady wage. He carved flutes but never sold them as artifacts. The sounds of a flute, he told me, were the sounds of nature and never an academic sideline or a tourist product.

My grandfather carved several cedar or sumac flutes in the summer, and he played the new flutes when the houseboat was docked near the headwaters. He sold the flutes only to people who could create music, but never to collectors. The sound of a native flute restored the presence of nature. The birch bark scrolls were not the same. We created and sold scrolls because they were images and stories, the shared scenes of native irony. The sound of the flute was the union of nature and totemic associations.

My grandfather refused to work for the government, or any related government agency, or for timber demons and grafters on the reservation. My grandmother, by her steady mood, native purchase, wit, and courage, nourished and maintained the family by chance, by poker booty, and by other visionary means.

Quiver was inspired by trickster stories of natural reason, but she was a reader, not a storier. She was serious about natural reason and survivance, intuitive and almost reverent about games of chance, and yet she explained that there was nothing unnatural about the poses, pretence, and strategic moves and simulations of a serious poker game.

Captain Eighty was a master of natural motion and the moods of nature. He taught my grandmother precise creature moves, the turns, waves, and quiver of leaves, the double teases and triple feigns, and by cunning eye tics, flutters and spurs, faint seductive wheezes, and finger trembles, to easily win a hand of poker. Yet he was a storier and never played games of chance with teachers or federal agents. My grandfather was a natural at the casual turn of trickster stories and the imagic scenes of memory.

Quiver became a visceral poker player, the marvelous mistress of poker games on the houseboat, at resort docks and tourist harbors, moorage near the headwaters, and at the federal agency. She played the lucrative games with a sense of chance and feigns of certainty. Most of the losers were over-the-counter weary federal agents.

True, she insisted that the children of the houseboat learn the strategies of instinctive resistance. The evasive dance of the killdeer, for instance, a course in natural reason, but she warned that once the pattern of the diversions and dance became familiar to the predators the survivance game was over for the plaintive plover.

Flush, my father, was never a plover, but he warned me with similar stories of natural reason and survivance. He cautioned me to never be unreserved or entirely known, no matter the practice, by a single pretence, sham, tactic, feign, gesture, or natural deceptive motions of an eye or hand. Change the strategies of survivance, the very nature of resistance, and the stories of the game. The stories of tricksters and seasons are elusive, imagic diversions, and memorable ironies of resistance, the native tease and feign of catchy survivance games.

Quiver learned more than one tricky wheeze, sneeze, hand move, and eye tic to win a poker hand from the predators of the game—federal agents, teachers, and others eager to beat a native woman at almost any cost. She raised, checked, and folded by decisive moves, and won at poker by the elusive tease of natural motion. She created a native sense of presence at the game and was unbeatable. My grandmother delegated the stories of natural reason and survivance to the native captains of the houseboat, Captain Eighty and then to her grandson Captain Carbon and later Captain Shammer.

Quiver lived alone on the Red Lust, summer and winter, for many years after the death of my grandfather. She was lonesome for the tease and humor, but secure with nineteen years of marvelous stories and erotic memories on the houseboat. My grandmother was never a shamanic healer of animals or birds, but abandoned and wounded mongrels continued to gather at the shoreline to be rescued for service on the houseboat. She continued that natural practice to honor the memory of the old trickster of the headwaters, Captain Eighty. Monte, Pope Pius, and Moby Jean reigned over the new mongrels of the waves.

Captain Shammer became the summer master of the creaky helm, the only grandchild who carried on the tease and manner of Captain Eighty. Quiver continued the poker games, and the active trade in inscribed birch bark scrolls. She was seldom alone or without a game because the tourists returned to the resorts in the summer and continued the traditions of poker on the anchored houseboat near the headwaters of the Mississippi River.

Captain Shammer wisely named our grandmother the first director of the Institute of Feigns and Games at the Full House Casino inaugurated in the former William Warren Memorial Library. Slash and Burn, bemused by the nomination on a birch bark scroll, read to his colleagues over lunch at the faculty club the fanciful inscription of the memorial library conversion to a casino. The deans and senior faculty at the high table were silent for a moment, a very precious academic moment, and then they burst into wild laughter. They were truly astounded that natives might survive with a casino and poker games at the university.

Slash and Burn considered many of the birch bark edicts in this way, a dramatic reading at the high table, and later he reported that three members of the faculty senate had saluted the innovation of an academic casino on campus. Actually, the salute was academic irony, in a sense, because the faculty senate had never rebuked or censured the eccentric actions, the peculiar gestures, or downright wacky pronouncements of native faculty in the Department of Native American Indian Studies.

Captain Shammer was a windward storier.

The chairmen of many other departments at the university petitioned the dean for permission to initiate similar casino games. Slash and Burn responded favorably by establishing the

Committee on Chance and Games to investigate the potential for academic theme casinos, the figuration of slot machine dials, roulette wheels, and black jack tables by disciplines, such as history, literature, political science, anthropology, chemistry, and physics. The academic disciplines are much more relevant than the fruit dials of cherries and oranges. The dean pointed out that poker, blackjack, and crap games, after all, are critical academic subjects of history, politics, psychology, and literature.

The ironic faces of selected distinguished scholars in these disciplines—for instance, Francis Parkman, N. Scott Momaday, John Locke, Karl Marx, Enrico Fermi, J. Robert Oppenheimer, and others—would be pictured on the three dials of slot machines. Political science would feature the faces of John Locke, Thomas Hobbes, and Karl Marx on their departmental slot machine dials. Franz Boas, Alfred Kroeber, and Ruth Benedict would likewise be winning faces on the anthropology slot machines.

The Full House Casino slot machines pictured Sitting Bull, Geronimo, White Cloud, Chief Joseph, Little Crow, and only a faint shroud of Crazy Horse. The jackpots were three images of a single native on the dials, and the grand winners were three shrouds of Crazy Horse.

The dean of dentistry proposed a bank of electronic slot machines in the waiting room of the clinic. Precise images of molars, incisors, impacted wisdom teeth, huge dental caries, and the perfect smiles of dental implants were pictured on the dials of the slot machines. The winners, three similar dental images on a dial, were awarded a free filling or extraction. The casino machines on campus were calibrated to lose only about three percent of the time.

Wiindigoo six card stud was a native discipline.

Quiver observed four great epochs of memory that autumn of

her career as an instructor and director of the Institute of Feigns and Games. She inspired an extraordinary sense of presence at the university by her interrelated epochs of memory. The epochs were inspired by natural reason, and every epoch memory was directly connected to a season, the traces of nature, raucous ravens over the headwaters, motion of red pine, or the crack of ice on the lake. The epochs were visual scenes of recounted memories from various perspectives. The epochs were related to historical events, situations, and the chance of dates, but the stories of the epochs were never the same.

Quiver revealed the first epoch of memory on the nuptial houseboat—the tease of my grandfather and manner of maritime mongrels, poker games with underhanded federal agents, and a sense of worldly presence—as a source of family and cultural knowledge. The epochs were enhanced by the coincidence of summer tourists and their stories.

The second epoch was the memory of my young aunt, Full House, who drowned in a wicked summer storm on Lake Itasca and washed ashore on August 6, 1945, the very same day that Little Boy, the first atomic bomb, destroyed the city of Hiroshima.

The third epoch of recounted memories was an association of literature, the perils of nuclear war, and a melancholy requiem on October 22, 1964, the incredible day the Mississippi River silently died near the University of Minnesota. Jean-Paul Sartre, on that very same day, refused to accept the Nobel Prize for Literature.

Quiver associated dates and stories, the intense moments of cultural perception, the turn of seasons, and even the style of clothes in catalogs. She remembered the Cuban Missile Crisis that brought the United States and Soviet Union close to war over the installation of missiles in Cuba. President John F. Kennedy declared on October 22, 1962, "It shall be the policy of this nation to regard any nuclear missile launched from Cuba against any nation in the Western Hemisphere as an attack on the United States, requiring a full retaliatory response upon the Soviet Union." That was an epoch of memory. The nuclear crisis ended, after a naval blockade, two weeks later, at the same time my aunt, Full House, was introduced to federal agents at poker games on the White Earth Reservation.

The fourth epoch, a heartfelt visionary connection and promise that one day Full House would manage a houseboat casino, was achieved by stories and the crucial presence of native memories. Full House had learned how to feign, wheeze, and bluff next to her mother at poker games with teachers, friendly tourists, and federal agents. Quiver, by the rush of epoch memories, became the teacher and manager of a casino in the name and memory of her beloved daughter.

The Full House Casino was a lucky native epoch of memories, and the most active and prosperous new program in the Department of Native American Indian Studies. The senior faculty and the failed chairmen of private office treaties were actually inspired by the spirited scenes and conversion of the native library into a casino. By the end of the semester the faculty had reversed their wearisome protests and participated in the communal feigns and games of poker. Straightaway over chance and a hand of cards the faculty renounced the sentiments of academic treaty rights of privacy, and instead celebrated survivance. The faculty embraced poker games, the traditional communal practices of moccasin games, songs, shams, teases, feigns, ironic stories, and the entrepreneurial adventures of higher education.

The faculty poker games became very popular on the campus, and some derivative games were scheduled at the faculty club. The Moccasin Games and most of the academic poker games

were held at the new Full House Casino, the former William
Warren Memorial Library. My grandmother never lost a hand of
academic poker, but even so there was a waiting list of potential
faculty players.

The Moccasin Games, a revived native tradition since the fur
trade, were once the sacred hand games of ancient memory. The
games, accompanied by the sound of hand drums and original
spirited gambling songs, teased, enticed, and beguiled the players. The traditional games were played with four moccasins, but
my grandmother introduced the use of square pieces of soft
deerskin decorated with elaborate beaded floral patterns. Four
objects, once bullets, metal objects, or coins, were hidden under
the moccasins. One of the bullets or objects was marked, and
the object of the game was to locate the hidden marked bullet.
The songs tempted the hunter of the hidden bullet to choose a
loosing moccasin.

Quiver continued to use new shiny bullets as the hidden objects, but she also introduced polished stones, and one of the four
stones was an agate. The stones were hidden under four squares
of leather. My grandmother taught the native students how to
beat the drum and to create original moccasin game songs. The
students were hesitant, even shied at first, but once the games
were underway the excitement of the drumbeats overcame any
unease or native reserve about the spirited play.

Captain Shammer wore moccasins.

The regular faculty poker players and steady losers at the Full
House Casino were Raymond Shove, professor of library science;
Tom Bard Jones, professor of history; John Turner, professor of
political science: David Noble and Mary Turpie, professors of
American studies; Franz Montgomery and Chester Anderson,
professors in the English Department, and the inimitable John

Wild, a truly wild and marvelous medical doctor. Edward Copeland, the one unshakeable and disciplined card folder who never
lost more than his ante in a game, was the Clement Professor
of Japanese Art and Literature.

Captain Shammer was never a poker player but he roamed
around the games from time to time in various masks. The
faculty players were not an austere chorus of the game, but the
shamanic masks carved by my father distracted some of the
serious gamblers. Besides the wooden masks my cousin wore
four synthetic baroque masks that resembled Jay Silverheels,
Sacheen Littlefeather, Jamake Highwater, and Jimmie Durham.
Silverheels, a native actor, played Tonto the trustworthy sidekick
of the Lone Ranger. Littlefeather, a native activist, became famous
as a proxy for Marlon Brando at the Academic Awards. Brando
had spurned the Best Actor Award for *The Godfather*, a curious
gesture to support the American Indian Movement occupation
of Wounded Knee, South Dakota. Highwater, or Jay Marks, was
a modern dancer and native poseur, a native by concession. The
masks and manners amused the faculty. Shammer sported at
times a golden badge with the fluorescent legend, Postmodern
Lippard *Sauvage*, when he wore the mask of Durham. My cousin
sometimes roamed around the games in the masks of faculty
members. The mask that distracted and troubled the faculty
more than any other was of John Berryman, the potent poet
and professor who had committed suicide by jumping from a
bridge over the Mississippi River.

Shove, an obsessive pick nitty and calculator of the cards,
never won by the scrutiny of numbers. Jones, a classical historian and the rumored recruiter of covert intelligence agents,
noticed faces, frowns, hand and shoulder gestures, but never
won a game by his studies of tics and body motions. Jones

was captivated by the secrecy of my grandmother, but he never seemed to notice her feigns and poker pretence. David Noble was the most inspired player at the games. He would closely examine the cards, slowly raise his head, close his eyes, and conduct the motion of the universe with a single card in his hand, and declare creative and critical comments about nations, pardons, wavers of elected politicians, and the ironic turns of history. Once or twice a month in the winter he would play his hand fully reclined on a seminar table, to favor the tender muscles of his back. No one remembers how much he won or lost at the poker games, but the prompts and teases of his cultural and political stories were truly memorable. Mary Turpie, always distracted by the character of the game and persona of the players, constantly urged my grandmother to consider a graduate program in American Studies. John Turner, a bully player, who always carried a bundle of maps, raised the stakes as he raised his voice over the games, higher and higher, and he lost more money than any other player. Franz Montgomery, emeritus faculty, was a steady player, a conservative bragger who closely watched the turn of every card. He was tormented by the chance of the game and lost every hand of poker. Franz scrupulously noted the pattern of cards and moves of the players in decorative hardbound blank books with deceptive titles, *War and Peace, Moby Dick,* and his favorite novel, *The Grapes of Wrath* by John Steinbeck. My grandmother constantly teased him about the titles of the blank books he carried. She actually asked the professor many times to sign blank books for her grandsons Dogroy Beaulieu and Captain Shammer.

Franz Montgomery was a blank book fancier.

Chester Anderson, who quoted passages from *Ulysses* and *Dubliners,* was the only faculty member to almost win a hand when my grandmother was in the game. Quiver closely observed his tender moves, the mercy of his smile, generous sense of humor, and folded her cards when he started to quote James Joyce. Chester recited by memory selections from *Ulysses* in a lusty resonate voice: "A man of genius makes no mistakes. His errors are volitional and are the portals of discovery." Later in the game when cold finger food was served to the players he quoted from *Dubliners*, "God made food; the devil the cooks." Chester Anderson was the first man of literature at the native poker games that my grandmother would listen to since the death of Captain Eighty.

Edward Copeland, a professor of haiku literature and the art of the floating world of woodblock prints, contributed an ante to every game, and nothing more. He secretly raised the corners of his cards, checked in turn, and then folded with the first raise. The cost of the ante was for the pleasure of the game and fair company. Copeland remarked that the senior faculty rarely gathered together without a committee of conspiracies, or academic apologies to share a casual chitchat, and in this instance, by chance of a poker game. He first discovered that liberal sense of communal presence as a translator in the military, later among natives, and when the casino opened in the library, in the company of his colleagues over a hand of wiindigoo six card stud.

Quiver created an original card game to torment the federal agents on the White Earth Reservation. The agents had taunted my grandmother that native cultures had never invented a memorable game of chance. Obviously the agents had never heard of the traditional Moccasin Game. Quiver won hand after hand and then declared that the Anishinaabe had actually created the game of five card stud. Later she provided evidence, obscure coins from the ancient monkery, to prove that natives had played the game five centuries ago with Benedictine monks at the Fleury sur Gichiziibi Monastery near the headwaters of the Mississippi River.

Wiindigoo six card stud is played with a standard deck of poker cards. Each player receives two cards down and four rounds of cards up with bets after each card is dealt. At the end, after the final round of cards and bets, the deck is shuffled, cut twice, and then the dealer turns over the card on the top of the secured deck. This is the wiindigoo card, the last card, and if that card is a king, queen, or jack, the same face cards in any hand of a player are dead and obsolete. So, for instance, if a player was dealt a queen down, and one queen up, and the last card turned was a queen, that royal card in the hand was obsolete, a wiindigoo card. The queens were dead and the player would lose the pair. Quiver declared that the chance of natives to win is always greater without the face cards of royalty. The origin of this poker game of diminished and obsolete royalty was inspired by natural reason, a native sense of chance, and, of course, by the fierce antimonarchist monks at the Benedictine Fleury sur Gitchiziibi Monastery.

Copeland wrote marvelous haiku poems between poker hands and presented them to my grandmother at the end of every game. Quiver was distracted, at times, by the voices of literature and haiku at casino poker. She mistrusted the federal agent on the reservation, and was amused by many of the goodhearted tourists who played poker on the houseboat near the headwaters, but these experiences were never tender distractions. Chester Anderson had an evocative and lusty voice that seemed to linger in her memory long after the games. David Noble was moved by the gestures of the haiku, but the other players would not be troubled, bemused, or distracted from the games.

poker hands
turn with the seasons
heart by heart

native player
quivers over the cards
ravens preen

The other perpetual faculty losers, similar to the bullies and federal agents on the reservation, were confident that one day they could outwit the old native woman at poker. Quiver easily encouraged and buoyed the spurious confidence of both the federal and faculty losers. Michel Baudrillard, one of the early faculty poker losers, a professor of French literature, announced a new nickname for my grandmother, the Five Hearts Woman.

Baudrillard explained that the esoteric nickname was derived from one of the early designers of the four suits and colors of playing cards. The French designer was inspired by the courage of Jeanne d'Arc at the Siege of Orléans, and he changed the image of a soldier on a deck of cards to the depiction of Jeanne d'Arc. Actually my grandmother won several hands of poker one night at the faculty club with a heart flush, and since then the stories of her nickname have become a romantic legend, the Five Hearts Woman.

Feigns, feathers, and avian names.

Quiver taught me how to play poker on the houseboat, but she never favored me to win, or any other grandchild, not even a hand of sympathy. I was seven years old at the time and she beat me seven times in a row with a flush. She displayed her cards for only two of the winning hands, hearts and spades. The other hands were never revealed, and they could have been a flush. The poker games that summer have become an epoch of memory.

Quiver first animated five wooden puppets to teach the native students the tricky motions, gestures, and strategies of poker, and then she invited the students to practice the tease, manner, and feigns in an actual poker game. The slow maneuvers of puppets were more theatrical and memorable than the motion and pictures of humans at the game. The imitations of the puppet moves were more original, clever, subtle, and the gestures were not shied by the visual memory of human actions. The puppet moves are imagined, eccentric, and not as easy to read as the imitations of most human motions.

Some of the students were humiliated at first by the puppets, and resisted the notion of juvenility. My grandmother was very persuasive, however, and overcame the morose and nervous humor when she introduced the students to several wooden masks of native ceremonials. Flush, my father, had carved the masks from white pine, and painted the rough faces with bold natural hues. The masks created a sense of native presence, and when the students wore the masks they were transformed by the power of a shamanic portrayal.

☞ 5 ☜

Panic Hole Chancery

The Baron of Patronia shouted at bears, public health nurses, federal agents, timber grafters, and the missionaries at the parish house, but his roar and natural thunder never changed the culture or party weather of the White Earth Reservation.

Captain Eighty told me that he might have been a panic hole shouter, but he was an earthdiver, a native storier of natural reason and refused to live on a treaty reservation. My grandfather never compromised his sense of survivance and continental liberty, and he would never curry favor with political toadies or the patronage of reservation politicians. Resistance to the government and federal agencies on the reservation had become an aesthetic practice.

The Baron of Patronia created panic holes.

Captain Eighty rushed the waves.

Patronia was a natural crescent on a meadow northeast of Bad Medicine Lake. The Baron and other visionary natives have

heard shamanic rumors of the ancient course of the great gla-
ciers near that meadow, and some natives have secured a native sense of presence and stories inspired by memories of the
ancient Lake Agassiz.

The Baron of Patronia built a cabin in the white pine near the
meadow. He shouted into panic holes and the meadow turned
blue with flowers. He was a healer by shouts, and the meadow
bloomed with the ancient roar. The Baron coached his children to
holler and scream into panic holes and the meadow was covered
with sturdy flowers, nurtured by their natural sounds. Even the
mongrels barked into panic holes. The earth awaits the roar of
bears and shouts of natives in the spring.

Baron was a nickname, a natural sense of nobility, but not by
status, birth, or descent. The tender rush of spring, the flush of
early flowers, and the blues, the waves of summer blues were
his barony. He was the lord of many panic holes on that glorious meadow. The earth was richer for his wild shouts, and
the blooms were brighter, copious, and fancy. The spectacular
flowers attracted many tourists to that particular meadow in
the summer. Floral scenes, natural reason, the survivance of
native traditions, and humane trickster stories were scarcely
conceivable without panic holes.

Captain Shammer was a houseboat sailor and he shouted
into the blue rush of waves, and the waves were bluer on Lake
Itasca near the headwaters of the Mississippi River. The Baron of
Patronia, panic holes, and bright flowers on the meadow, came
to mind that morning when my cousin decided to convert the
private faculty offices to native practices. The hollers and roars
of natives were natural, and the students would learn the art of
survivance by the necessary shouts into panic holes.

The Panic Hole Chancery was decorated with soundproof

material to prompt, accommodate, and encourage student shout-ers, and to provide a secure location for an elusive native radio station. Captain Shammer invited Panic Radio, a covert late night radio station for native shouters in a panic, to broadcast without notice from the university. Panic Radio was portable, not licensed, and at times the station broadcasts were at river colonies, native bars, over onions and sturdy hamburgers at the Band Box Diner, and on a bench at Elliot Park near downtown Minneapolis.

Panic Radio featured overnight native shouts, hollers, ironic roars, and penury curses that were potent, crucial, and actual, far from a reservation or meadow of panic holes, but nonethe-less wild in the night air of the city. Natives at the river colonies shouted over the poisoned shoreline, shouted into cardboard boxes, barrels, and yelled into restaurant dumpsters on Panic Radio.

Captain Shammer inaugurated the new Panic Hole Chancery with a public competition of urban bellowers and shouters. Three senior native faculty members who had barely subdued their rage over the termination of private offices were ready to curse with impunity the new chairman and the university. Many professors from discrete academic departments—anthropology, literature, philosophy, library science, linguistics, and history—were eager to register in the first tournament of university shouters.

Panic Radio announced the competition every night for more than two weeks, and the number of registrations by community shouters reached more than seventy, nine from the river colonies alone, and many more from the dumpster yellers.

The tournament became much too large to contain in the converted faculty office. Shammer secured a huge magisterial lecture room in the law school for the event. Several hundred people were registered for the tournament in the end, so the shouters were scheduled to compete in several heats in the lecture room, and in front of an audience. Seven judges were selected by my cousin to determine the winner of the tournament. Shammer named three native military veterans, a retired high school football coach, two women soccer trainers, and an auctioneer. The ten best shouters competed in the final roars at the Panic Hole Chancery.

Harry Manner, one of the most harried native yellers in the city, was declared the winner of the first tournament of shouters by the unanimous decision of the judges. He had been a student of political science for more than a decade, but the graduate committee denied his dissertation. Harry turned to shouts and marched through the campus and circled the downtown everyday for more than seven years. His huge voice was heard in winter classrooms, the university hospital, and even in the stacks of the main library. Harry marched and shouted daily about state government, about war, any war, about the faculty and the university, the Bureau of Indian Affairs, the Department of Justice, and he shouted in a military stride about the United States Army.

Harry auditioned for the tournament with a huge shout about nuclear arms and the Cold War, won the first heat with a bellowed imitation of *Fever* by Peggy Lee, a popular song of the sixties, and he was victorious in the final competition of the tournament with an intense original rant and rave of the King James Version of Psalm 23. "The Lord is the shepherd of my voice. I shall not want more than one meal a day. He maketh me lie down in green pastures, but only on the reservation. He leadeth me beside the paths of righteousness in his name not mine. Yea, though I walk through the valley of the shadow of death in political science at the university, I will fear no evil, for thou art with me, my rod and thy staff they comfort me. . . . Surely goodness and mercy shall follow me all the days of my life. I will dwell under the bridge with men who say they are the lords of the cardboard and dumpsters."

The students were inspired by the wanton and unrestrained shouters at the tournament, and practiced their shouts and signature roars in the Panic Hole Chancery. Crucial declarations from the Fort Laramie Treaty, selected dialogue from western movies, *Cheyenne Autumn*, *Broken Arrow*, and *Stay Away, Joe*, with Elvis Presley, were shouted over simulated panic holes.

Captain Shammer expected the students to shout their rage over the ironic narratives of treaties, selections from reports by missionaries on federal reservations, and other derogatory doctrines and documents of dominance, but he was astonished that the native student shouters were wild about poetry, especially the lyrical scenes by the mysterious Wendy Rose. The poems were magical in any tone of voice, resonance, tender whisper, or by roars and shouts.

The Chant Shouters, the name the students created in a rage, performed a new literary convention. The rehearsal shouts, roars, and bellows were operatic, in the tradition of the rhythmic chant and chorus of "Happy We!" in *Acis and Galatea*, a pastoral opera by George Frideric Handel. The student chants and shouts were intense, lively, and spirited, a drum beat shout, a native tease, but not with any trace of trickster ridicule.

The Chant Shouters evoked by their operatic shouts and hollers a passionate resonance and shamanic conversion of native literature. The native students chanted and shouted a few lines from a marvelous poem, "If I Am Too Brown or Too White For You," by Wendy Rose:

remember I am a garnet woman
whirling into precision
as a crystal arithmetic. . . .

The Chant Shouters of the Panic Hole Chancery were encouraged to continue with a shout, bellow, and roar of "The Man from Washington," an ironic poem about a "crude beginning" by James Welch:

The end came easy for most of us. . . .

The Chant Shouters were inspired by the haiku poet Patrice Beaulieu, and by Dylan Thomas, the poet and author of *Portrait of the Artist as a Young Dog.* The haiku poems and native erotic images were much easier to chant shout than most other poetry.

spring fever
basho wades in the shallows
cranes arise

mounds of foam
downriver from the waterfall
float silently

The Chant Shouters, a party of seven native students, practiced the chant shout of one particular poem over and over for several months at the Panic Hole Chancery. The students were determined to present the poem, "Do Not Go Gentle into That Good Night" by Dylan Thomas, at the first graduation ceremony of the shouters and new department.

Do not go gentle into that good night. . . .
Rage, rage against the dying of the light. . . .

The Chant Shouters roared the rage, rage of the poem, and inspired some listeners of Panic Radio. The river colonies were moved by the shouts of rage against the death of natural light and natives. The sunrise glanced over the river in the summer, and at night the lights were turned out across the dead water at the university. The last wave and shimmer of light died every night in the river. Two of the shouters once lived in the river colonies. They were the natural chanters of rage and the dying light.

The Chant Shouters, a few months later, shouted on radio, night after night, the entire ten comic autobiographical stories in the *Portrait of the Artist as a Young Dog* by Dylan Thomas.

 6

Irony Dogs

Dean Slash and Burn visited the department late that autumn concerned about reports that stray and vagrant mongrels were attending lectures and barking at professors. The dean was in doubt that the determined barkers were the actual irony dogs in advanced training at the university.

The doggy disruption of lectures became the subject of serious ruminations at the deanery and over lunch at the faculty club. The regents had proclaimed that dogs were not permitted on campus, except, of course, for canine service companions and the deserted mongrels directly involved in terminal scientific research in the dental and medical schools.

Captain Shammer waited at the elevator and escorted the dean and two nervous subordinates to the communal faculty conference room for a formal discussion of animals on the campus. My cousin anticipated that the university would order the removal of mongrels, so he prepared a petition to secure the natural rights of animals, and to protect mongrels at the university. He informed the dean that native scientific studies of mongrel practices to uncover the absence of irony were critical to any sense of academic liberty.

The irony mongrels were ironic service dogs.

Shammer described the original native activities and practices in each of the seven offices vacated by the faculty. Madeline Seams, two senior faculty, several graduate students, and irony dogs trailed the dean and his nervous party down that extraordinary hallway of uncertainty and adventure. That hallway of panic holes and irony dogs was unlike any academic enterprise in the history of the university.

Slash and Burn was intrigued by the trade names of the new enterprise disciplines in the department. He pointed at the unique signboards and read out loud the names with an incredulous tone of voice: Panic Hole Chancery, Irony Dogs, Skin Dunk, Last Lecture, Postindian Holograms, Denivance Press, Stray Visions, and the proposed center of original native arts, Cavalier Rouge. The dean was obsessed with the connotations, metaphors, and substance of the names. Eventually he worried more about the name of the Panic Hole Chancery, the nature of Skin Dunk, and Stray Visions, than he did about the Irony Dogs.

The deanery subordinates were distracted by native chants and shouts overheard near the Panic Hole Chancery. They hurried past the irony mongrels, the very cause of the negative reports on campus, and the principal reason for the departmental visit. Three mongrels posed, panted, and smiled on the threshold of the new center for the education of Irony Dogs.

Chance lived with many, many mongrels on the reservation and later at the Gallery of Irony Dogs located in the First Church of Christ Scientists in Minneapolis. Dogroy, my cousin, painted baroque portrayals of natives in the organic orange light of the stained glass church windows. Chance, at the same time, nurtured and coached the mongrels at the back of the studio for irony duty. Every story, gesture, portrayal, name, appointment, and confession was an ironic signature in the creative worlds of Chance and Dogroy.

Captain Shammer had invited Chance to provide advanced training for the irony mongrels at the university, and so one of the faculty offices was reserved for the mongrels to practice the art of irony perception and the absence of academic irony. Chance, one of the many Women of the Creature Arts associated with Dogroy, was never at ease in the company of men. She would sooner share the favors of mongrels than the casual attention of men. Chance would certainly not enter the gender competition of men and women.

Chance learned as a child that mongrels were healers and she was convinced that the originary bark of a mongrel heard around the world was a natural and astute response to the absence of humor and irony among insecure hunters, wasteland truth seekers, terminal devotees, and imperial monsters. Naturally, the first mongrel barkers over irony were healers. Some of these early mongrels of irony migrated with the mercenaries of truth and the crackpots of fundamentalism. The primeval mongrels of irony learned to bark with caution at savages, sovereigns, and heritage poachers. The mongrels always barked at holy guile and the absolute sincerity of Christianity.

The monotheists forever separated animals as lowly creatures, as an unconnected creation, absent a soul or salvation, and with no godly significance as healers. Even so the trusty mongrels persisted to bark and warn the world that the absence of irony is terminal and the treacherous end of civilization.

Chance trained the mongrels to attend lectures and to bark at the absence of irony. Naturally, the students who were bored by forthright narratives and absolute sincerity appreciated the diversion of a hearty bark. The bark was a serious point, and the irony dogs barked at almost every lecture, an obvious declaration of the absence of academic irony.

Captain Shammer told Slash and Burn that the irony dogs were shaman healers, and warned the dean that the absence of irony can only bring about the sooty remains of governance. So, my cousin declared that the faculty should imitate the barks of the mongrels to save the university from the absence of irony.

Slash and Burn was not a service animal.

Shammer was a tricky storier, and he easily out shamed the abusers of natural reason in a shame game culture. He told the dean that mongrels were misused, abused, and exterminated in research programs at the university. Not even a pretentious shame culture would protect the mongrel healers, and yet the mongrels prevailed and continued to bark around the world at the absence of irony in science and cultural studies at the university.

Slash and Burn was an accountant, not a scientist, and he was not an animal enthusiast either, but he endured with a sense of humor the lectures on animal protection and ethics. Shammer told stories about the sacrifice of mongrels at the university dental school in a study to determine the best surgical procedures to connect and heal a broken jawbone. My cousin learned about the mongrel miseries from a native who once worked as a research assistant, and who never fully recovered from the traumatic memories of hoarse, croaky mongrels in the laboratory. The native assistant nicknamed every trusty mongrel in the jawbone experiment. General Brown, Hunky, Nail Biter, Lucky Jane, Droopy, Big Foot, and Top Tail were honored in name and song at the final moment of extermination by lethal injections of sodium pentothal.

The dental surgeon retrieved mongrels that were detained for more than two weeks and sentenced to death in animal shelters. The surgeon severed the vocal folds to silence the mongrels. Daily these brave mongrels of liberty continued to warn the world about the absence of irony, but only with a raspy trace of a bark. My cousin wondered if the barks around the world were a tribute in memory of those loyal raspy barkers.

The surgeon anesthetized the mongrels, broke their jawbones with his hands, and then secured the bones by various methods, wires, screws, and by other means to determine the most effective surgical procedures on humans with broken jawbones. Top Tail was the last of the research mongrels to be exterminated with a broken jawbone at the university.

Top Tail was a raspy mongrel warrior.

Derrida arrived at the conference room with two other irony dogs. He leaped onto a faculty desk and gently barked at the two subordinates. Turnip and Nixon leaped onto nearby faculty desks and sneezed several times, the manner of restrained barks over the absence of irony. Slash and Burn was amused by the scene, and grateful that the mongrels had not found him lacking in ordinary academic irony.

Derrida was invited to hear the dean and his subordinates explain the tedious and bigoted reports on mongrel barks. The mongrel philosopher was considered a member of the native faculty, and he was there in the conference room to represent native reason and mongrel liberty, the rights of animals to bark at professors who lecture with deadly sincerity, and to honor the memory of the many research mongrels that were exterminated at the university.

Derrida, Turnip, and Nixon bounced on the faculty desks and barked at every use of the word "bark" in the reports, barked at every verb, and barked louder at the institutional adjectives that denied mongrel liberty, the native mongrel rights to bark at deadly sincerity, and the terminal lectures that would weaken stories of survivance and civilization. The three advanced mongrels barked without restraint at the absence of irony.

Slash and Burn folded his arms and turned away.

Derrida bayed at the liberal academic slights, the stay of apologies, manifest manners, and the deferred sense of autocracy. Derrida growled even louder at the hand gestures of academics, and deconstructed by snarls the historical concert of dominance and separatism. Then he bounced on his four black paws, the pied noir of irony dogs, and barked in slow muffled bursts at the silence of the dean, the shy, twitchy subordinates, and the agents of arbitrary despotism over native mongrel liberty.

Slash and Burn capitulated the very next day when Captain Shammer declared that if the prohibition of mongrels on the campus and at lectures were not removed he would summon the shamans of six reservations, and with thousands of irony mongrels, converge at the university faculty club. My cousin emphasized that the barks of the mighty mongrel would be truly memorable and heard around the world in the absence of irony and mongrel liberty at the University of Minnesota.

Slash and Burn was worried mostly that the native casino and other academic entrepreneurial ventures would be moved to another university, so he immediately absolved the critical nature of the reports and abolished forever the denial of mongrel rights to bark at deans, faculty, students, and the absence of irony, or to bark at the moon and winter wiindigoo at the university.

☞ 7 ☜

Skin Dunk

Old Darkhorse was the ingenious founder of a timely and necessary postindian bodily hue and colorant service. The Half Moon Bay Skin Dunk was an essential application for many urban natives, and much later for primarily native nationalists. The skin dunks were inaugurated in the quaint town of the same name in northern California.

Darkhorse produced a secret character concoction of herbs, roots, twigs, bark, fish bone, and the bile of wolverines, a fermented sauce that changed the color of ordinary human complexion. The only telltale signs of a skin dunk were slightly darker cuticles.

Captain Shammer summoned the prominent shaman of skin dunks and identity brews as a consultant to provide that singular service to natives in the department, and to others who favored the discrete pleasures of darker skin. Shammer observed that academic politics evolved with the color of skin, and that faculty dunks were directly related to more serious associations and promotions at the university.

The Skin Dunk center operated late at night in subdued light and only by appointment. Flying Colors or Skin Dunk was the obscure name printed on a simulated birch bark signboard over the former faculty office. Most of the skin dunk clients were secretive, a contradiction that indicated the insecurities of race and identity. The shy clients did not want to be seen emerging from the dunk center with the radiance of darker skin. My cousin told me that progressive white lie liberals with a lack of color confidence were the most frequent late night dunkers at the Flying Colors.

The immersion time in the brew was no more than thirty minutes, and the distinct color lasted for about six months by ordinary erosion and daily showers. The choice and intensity of the color determined the actual brew time. The only abuse of the service was a power dunk of three tipsy blondes after a wild party on the riverbank near the university. The police arrived an hour after the dunk and considered the incident a blonde moment because no one conceded or protested the evidence of color.

Captain Shammer declared that there was nothing new about the concept and practice of the color dunks because natives have forever blackened their hair for cosmetic authenticity, and overnight brunettes have become blondes. So, never mind, my cousin raved, that the body is a stretched canvas for distinctive tattoos. No, no, the body is a palette of complexions and substitute identities. Turn out the light and listen to the tone of a voice, an honor song, a tease, the stories of irony dogs, the glint of an eye, the erotic scent of sweat, and the generous touch of a lover to determine the praise of color and the pleasures of native identity.

Old Darkhorse, a native nickname that became a surname, was dark but not by the dunk. Old is an adjective, not his given name. He has no archived first or given name. No one doubted that he was native, and yet he was vague about his ancestors. He named various cultures and reservations as his home, family, and community. The inconsistencies about his native origins, the obvious sign of a poseur, were overlooked because he delivered an extraordinary service, a catchy ceremony of simulated complexion and identity.

Darkhorse created an enormous skin color circle of hues and tones to represent variations of complexion. The selections of skin hues were calculated by age, original color, weight, and time in the skin dunk. The actual procedure was mysterious, but the outcome of the skin dunks was memorable. The most favored complexion on the circle of hues was similar to the leather color of the inner bark of the birch tree. The same inner bark that natives used to create scrolls and to incise pictomyths and stories.

Captain Shammer was concerned that so many pasty liberal faculty members were secretly dunked by appointment. The faculty skins were radiant, of course, but the new complexion competed with the color of real natives. My cousin was about to report his concerns to the dean when two older professors, one in music and the other in geography, emerged from the dunk with marbled colored skin. The professors expected to recover a sandy complexion, but instead they were horrified by the mottled and marbled colors, even darker in the wrinkles.

Darkhorse explained that for some reason the wolverine bile coagulated in contact with certain natural oils in older skin. He explained that the marble bile coagulation was rare, though that was no comfort, and yet he convinced the two professors that in spite of the marbled tones their complexion was much more desirable than pale puckers and creases. The marbled skin dunk story circulated widely around the campus and scared the pale faculty.

Last Lecture

Father Mother Browne renounced his ordination and solemn vows as a priest, and his abandonment of the popery was done with no breach of peace or irony. He returned to the cedar manor and tavern near the reservation and decided to become a woman at his own Last Lecture.

Captain Eighty told me stories about the priest, or the woman, a trickster or a shaman, who reversed the traces of native character and the ordinary perceptions of reality. Father Mother created the tavern and the sensational convention of last lectures. Night after night two or three native fakers recited their exit stories at the tavern, a serious preparation to deliver one last earnest, tricky, and ironic lecture, and then vanished out the back with the vital documents of a new postindian identity.

Father Mother converted the sacred priestly confessionals and the sacraments of penance into a conspicuous last lecture, a secular revelation of getaway stories in a tavern. Mostly the confessions of remorse were tricky stories of native deceit and fakery. The notions and recitations of forgiveness were nothing more than the enthusiastic response of an audience and an exit strategy with an unused identity. The patrons at the tavern were taken aback one night when the priest waived his own clerical covenants and proclaimed in a last lecture that he would become a woman with a new postindian identity.

Father Mother forever grieved for the native dead at wakes, vigils, and many, many funerals. He told saintly stories about the dear departed natives, and then told naughty stories about the saints, a natural tease and turnaround of native solace. The priest habitually ate too many commodity cheese and peanut butter sandwiches with the survivors. Plainly the old native ladies were in love with the priest, and yet he had not worn a clerical collar in more than a decade. Some of the ladies were heartened that a priest could become a woman.

The fourteen constant parishioners heard his gentle sermons at the tiny church surrounded by the Way of Sorrows, or the Stations of the Cross. No one ever worried about the church turnout because more than a hundred parishioners heard his ironic stories nightly at the Last Lecture.

The Last Lecture was my pastime one summer.

Father Mother celebrated natural reason and the sensations of native irony in his tavern outside the reservation boundary to escape the inevitable shakedown of politicians. The tavern of priestly irony was located near the ruins of Fleury sur Gichiziibi, the ancient monastery, and the headwaters of the Mississippi River.

Father Mother wore many hats, a brown fedora, panama, cowboy, beret, mauve miter, and a red hard hat with the words "Postindian Pride" painted on the back when he introduced the confessants at the Last Lecture. The priest constructed the huge cedar tavern many years ago, and asked my father to carve the name of the Last Lecture on a huge beam over the entrance.

The Last Lecture was named for the last lectures.

The Oval Office, a notorious executive liquor bar at the center of the tavern, was encircled by a theater or lecture center where hundreds of native poseurs, losers, militants, spirit wasters, culture and heritage poachers, writers, teachers, misfits, and others delivered their memorable last lectures. The confessions and recollections of the last lecturers were heartfelt, crafty, wacky, treacherous, comical, pathetic, and yet the vents were always unintended irony. The poseurs and penitents, taunted by an eager audience of heavy drinkers, were provided at the end of the last lectures with a contrived postindian identity.

Captain Shammer moored the Red Lust several times that summer near the headwaters, and as a family we visited the Last Lecture. Moby Jean and the mighty maritime mongrels protected the houseboat from the ghosts of the nearby monkery. Pope Pius sensed the presence of the abused mongrels with two feathery tails. Monte was a hearty barker at the ghostly shadows on the move in the giant red pine at night.

Flush, my father, drank warm gin at the Oval Office on these occasions, and mocked the pretensions of the last lecturers in memory of Captain Eighty. Quiver played poker at a side table with eager tourists and confessants who were very anxious losers at cards. The grandchildren circled the tables and watched the tactical tics and feigns of the players. My grandmother taught me how to set an eye, and to anticipate the gestures of the game and tavern irony. We discovered a new world by the tricky and elaborate pretensions of native poseurs at the Last Lecture.

Coke de Fountain, the former pantribal cocaine dealer, was the only entrant who avowed his native scandals and then reneged on his solemn last lecture apparently because one tipsy patron at the bar shouted and cursed that the druggy was a hokey militant only for the money, a cheat and a faker of native traditions. The banality of fakery should not have been a distraction at a last lecture, but the unsteady patrons at the bar turned and stared in silence at the contemptible confessant and poseur at the lectern.

Coke had betrayed the very purpose of personal revelations at the Last Lecture with deceptive and overstated descriptions of his tedious mercenary adventures as a warrior during the occupation of Alcatraz, the former federal prison on a rocky island in San Francisco Bay, California. Sometimes the obvious ornamental stories and situations became a slander to serious drinkers in the Oval Office of the Last Lecture.

Marie Gee Praiseme, a native curriculum consultant for the public schools, conceded at a last lecture that she had promoted as cultural traditions the false notions that natives avoided eye contact and never touched, teased, or embraced another person. She had deceitfully reduced communal sentiments and the common practice of nickname teases to an invented no touch native tradition. The students at a reservation school assembly once snickered at her feeble philosophy, and then they burst into laughter when a newcomer raised his hand and asked the crackpot consultant if masturbation was a native tradition.

Marie Gee bemoaned the many fake traditions that she had advanced in the curricula of public education. Her last lecture was wholehearted, and a wacky, weepy performance. She was isolated by her own confession and in desperate want of a humane touch and instant mercy, a tradition pardon, and, of course, a new postindian identity.

Most of the last lectures were more in tune with the sentiments of concocted victimry than with the practices of native survivance. Father Mother had graciously accommodated over the years a huge number of pretentious native academics at the Last Lecture. Some of the academics rightly deserted their learned grievances at the Oval Office. The academics were moody drinkers at first, but they were heartened by the many earnest and ironic last lectures. The junior faculty boozers were envious of the confessants who earned original names and new postindian identities. The older professors with tenure, however, had too much to lose by the conversion.

The most pretentious native professors were at rest with cultural chauvinism, the peak ironic pose of a last lecture. These tedious doctrinaires favored ideology over research, theory, or creative literature. They simulated native traditions to oppose the notion of postindian conversions. The culturalists might have become natural confessants—academic poseurs, lazy-eye readers ready for a last lecture. They linger at the bar, bent on an easy fight over the mushy confessions and postindian sentiments.

Father Mother compared the native culturists to a motley band of grackles perched on a barbed wire fence. That sullen repose of the culture poachers was preparation for a revised last lecture, a faux lecture that would provide a secure ideological escape to postindian traditions and nationalism.

Homer Yellow Snow, the native novelist who arrived at the tavern in a brown limousine, revealed that he stole his many scenes, tropes, and dialogue concepts from diverse authors. Yellow Snow announced that he poached descriptive scenery, figures of speech, and copied entire sentences from novels by D'Arcy McNickle, John Joseph Mathews, N. Scott Momaday, Jack London, and John Steinbeck. His last lecture confessions of literary piracy surprised many people in the audience. That his obvious plagiarism went undiscovered until his last lecture suggested that there were not many close readers of native fiction. Yellow Snow might have actually faked his own last lecture and confession as a plagiarist, a desperate, and deceptive revelation merely to attract more attention as a native author.

These two native fakers and poseurs delivered memorable last lectures and then vanished with new names and original identities. Each participant in the last lectures was provided with a new name and essential documents of ingenious postindian identity. Charlotte, formerly Marie Gee, and Sonar, preconfession Homer, however, did not vanish without a trace after their last lectures. They were eager to adopt new names and original identities, and walk out the back door of the tavern into a new world, but they were not secure enough to be absolved confessant poseurs. They were clingers and stalked the former priest around the world. Charlotte and Sonar could not bear the anxiety of native liberty and became his unwanted apostles of the last lecture.

Father Mother Browne became Rosy Banish.

Captain Shammer located the former priest in San Gregorio, California. Rosy cultivated organic cabbages and Brussels sprouts at a ranch near the ocean. My cousin invited her to recreate the very same ironic practices and promise of postindian identities on the run in the Department of Native American Indian Studies. The common avowals would be more academic, but the same tavern conventions, with relevant documents and postindian names, as the priest had established at the Last Lecture near the headwaters of the Mississippi River would be resumed.

The Oval Office Library, the new name of the moveable academic bar, served only birch bark beer on the run. The students learned how to ferment birch bark and they secretly served a beer with alcohol. The income doubled from the sale of beer at the last lectures on campus.

Two urban poseurs were the first entrants at the inauguration of the departmental Gichi Giiwanimo Last Lecture. My cousin selected the Anishinaabe words *gichi*, or big, and *giiwanimo*, a lie, as the distinct name of the new or second Last Lecture. The actual terminal avowals were scheduled in the conference room and large lecture halls on the campus. Captain Shammer was certain that students and some faculty would be the best audiences for the last lectures, as they were already familiar with similar revelations in academic lectures and seminars.

Rafe Bear was the first confessant scheduled that autumn at the Gichi Giiwanimo Last Lecture. He was stout, dark, a stony native character, and smartly dressed for the lecture event. My cousin wore the LaDonna Harris mask that afternoon when he introduced the confessant as a wounded and decorated war veteran, a certified nurse with a degree from the University of California, Berkeley, and a doctorate with honors in clinical psychology from the University of Southern California.

The LaDonna mask heartened the audience.

Captain Shammer announced that Rafe Bear was hired by a local hospital, and with no verifiable credentials, to direct a clinical program for native alcoholics. My cousin was eager to remind the audience that the dean had appointed him to direct native studies without qualifications, but he never faked degrees or pretended to be an academic. Shammer was not a confessant but he told the audience that he had never attended or graduated from any school and that he never had a real interest in the university.

Rafe Bear moved slowly to the rostrum and leaned over the birch bark lectern, an awkward position for a huge man. He turned to the side, but never raised his head, and presented his entire last lecture with no eye contact. The audience was silent, deferential, and uneasy. He was sullen, reticent, and evasive, a native that actualized the very romance of natives simulated by progressive urban liberals. Bear was favored at dinner parties, and at courtly repasts he easily convinced the lords and ladies of his authenticity by references to nature and by the use of obscure metaphors. Natives were more veracious if they were dark, moody, and gentle emissaries of nature with hazy stories. The native fakers and poseurs were always ready to adapt to the cues of bounty and the enlightened charity of the aristocracy.

Bear actually surprised the audience in his first sentence. He declared that the doctorate and certificates noted in his resume were true and authentic. He paused, leaned closer to the microphone, and murmured with only the slightest smile that even his denials were believable. Bear had faked his own denial. That was a very tricky start of his last lecture, and he continued with his head turned and with no eye contact.

Sure, the liberals wanted me to be their fantastic professional Indian. How could they think otherwise? I only had to allow them to complete the stories they wanted to believe. The big lie was their anticipation of a certified warrior, and here we are at this historical big lie last lecture.

My resume was impressive, actually it was masterly, and most of you were dazzled when you should have turned me down as a faker. No, you made me, you needed a faker, and you wanted me to be a super Indian with a doctorate in clinical psychology. I was easier to relate to with terminal degrees. The universities that impressed you so much don't even offer degrees in nursing and clinical psychology.

I was never wounded or decorated.

My fakery would never have been exposed if the liberals had not been so eager to get an Indian elected to the school board. You see, to be a candidate for the school board required a fingerprint and inves-

tigation by the Federal Bureau of Investigation. Why not? Would you want a sex criminal elected to the school board? Not me. No one at that point had ever checked my credentials. I was exposed by that routine investigation, as you know, and that was a good thing. Newspaper reporters were tracking the doctors who hired me at the hospital. My presence was denied that very day, and with no goodbyes. I would still be your super Indian, faker or not, and it really didn't matter, did it, because I was great at being a clinical psychologist. I surely would have continued serving many Indian drunks who never saw me as a faker. I would be at the clinic today if only you had not wanted me to be more, to be the source of Indian wisdom on the school board, and in the very ruins of your own culture.

So, I am standing as the first confessor at the Gichi Giiwanimo Last Lecture, but my confession is not about a big lie. My poses are not a lie, and my clinical service is not a lie. I served Indian drunks at the hospital, and on weekends I performed for the liberals at dinner parties. My confession is really your confession. You created the fake Indians you needed to satisfy a liberal, sometimes even radical, consciousness about the guilt over the treatment of Indians in the United States.

Yes, you know, of course you know, how the pursuit of fake Indians got started. Your ancient relatives created the poseurs and started the fakery. Right, it was your kith and kin that concocted Indian chiefs to fake the treaties, and everyday dubious headmen were named in federal documents. Your ancestors even created shamans to shame as heathens and savages. So, this is your big lie, not mine. Your relatives shamed our healers and then appeased their guilt over stolen land and the removal of Indians to reservations. You have the real tradition of fakery, my dear friends, and that fakery is yours not mine. I only stepped in temporarily to satisfy your needs.

Farewell to the academics, farewell to you the founders and tra-

ditional sponsors of Indian poseurs and fakers, and remember that
every word you heard in my last lecture today was the truth, and
nothing but the truth, so help me liberals. Now it is time for me to
escape from your fakery with a new postindian identity.

Penelope Terreblanche Ford was the second confessant that
autumn at the Gichi Giiwanimo Last Lecture. She was a professor of literature at a community college, and had published
several critical studies on native poetry and novels, including
Native American Resurrection. She proclaimed that no scholar had
ever uncovered the avowed plagiarism of Homer Yellow Snow.

Captain Shammer quickly changed masks from LaDonna
Harris to Vine Deloria. The audience shouted high praise of the
author of *Custer Died for Your Sins* and *God is Red*. My cousin
was eager to schedule Terreblanche Ford, or Miss Easy, as the
second confessant because she was almost the perfect opposite
of the first confessant. Miss Easy was given that nickname by
native teasers on the reservation tribal council. Rafe Bear was a
faker of credentials but not his native identity. Miss Easy was a
white faker with a doctorate and earned credentials, a wannabe
native. Bear was native with a stance. Miss Easy was desperate
to be native.

Captain Shammer told the audience that Terreblanche Ford
was born near the White Earth Reservation. Her father served
for more than thirty years as a federal agent and built a huge
house on the shore of Bad Medicine Lake. Miss Easy lived near
natives in the summer, a seasonal association, and the rest of the
year she attended prestigious private schools. She studied native
cultures, material and ethereal, and native histories from rock
art to tricksters. She might have been a marvelous and clever
native, but not even an authentic erudite native would have been
received without a mighty tease. Miss Easy never had a chance

to be native, my cousin told the audience, but because she was so earnest and devoted to natives the tribal council named her in the language of the fur trade, Terre Blanche, or White Earth, the first of many nicknames. Miss Easy would not reveal the situations or private stories that resulted in her current nickname.

Miss Easy was native by association.

I could run faster, swim better, write stories, play the piano, and could name more trees, flowers, birds, animals, and insects than anyone around Bad Medicine Lake. That, however, was not enough to be native. I even hung around the nearby Boy Scouts of America summer camp to learn about the Order of the Arrow. I was truly overawed by the spectacle of the honor society, the traditions and ceremonies borrowed from natives. I know now, of course, that these were romantic simulations, but the notions were inspired by the advice of Charles Alexander Eastman. Even so, who would not want to be honored by the Order of the Arrow? That, as you can imagine, was a real mistake because my native friends gave me many nicknames, but the one that stuck for many years was none other than Eagle Scout. Several years later my native friends named me Miss Easy. I only accepted that name, never mind the real reasons for the name, because it was better at the time than Eagle Scout.

I know, this is the second last lecture on the campus, and you did not pay to hear me moan about my knowledge of birds and boy scouts. You want to hear some character dirt, singular deception and fakery. Yes, of course, the confessions of urgency, the last crucial revelations that give me cause to escape out the back door with a new postindian identity. That alone, the solemn promise of a postindian identity, would be enough motivation to fake anything.

I have always wanted to be an Indian. I am an Indian, lived like an Indian, did everything that Indians do on the reservation, but because my father was an Indian agent there was no chance for me to be accepted as an Indian. What was so wrong about a person who wanted to be an Indian? Indians ought to welcome my gestures and accept my honorable aspirations. Why do Indians resent my flights of fancy? I know, because there is always an escape distance in my desire to play the role.

I am a very determined person, as you can see, so my want to be an Indian changed course. My nicknames connected me to the fur trade and Indians, and my knowledge of Indians was recognized as a university student, so the critical pleasure of identity came to me with no real effort.

White Earth was a reservation and my nickname, and the rest was an obvious conclusion. Are you Indian? Well, the first time someone asked me that I turned away. Later, however, the question provided me with an easy discussion of my family home on the reservation, on the shore of Bad Medicine Lake. The assumption of my identity was natural, obvious, and remained unstated at the university. Who would have unique nicknames and come from the reservation and not be an Indian? So, my teachers and students made it easy for me to become an Indian. They made me an Indian. My teachers created a natural faker. Not a deceiver, in the active sense, but a serious person who could not resist what others expected of me as an Indian. And I was a very good one, always loyal to the cultural history of the White Earth Reservation. I have always been more knowledgeable about Indian cultural history than most of my Indian friends. So, who would not want someone like me to speak as an Indian?

You made me an Indian, and now you have become the paid witnesses of my escape from the great fakery of my identity. You made me the sort of Indian you wanted to know. I wanted to be a real Indian, not the passive simulation that comes with every image of Indians. I became the image of curiosity, and was never known as a unique and clever person. I only realized the personal distance of being an Indian at the time of my promotion to professor with tenure at the community college. My career as a teacher was some identity protection, at first, but my colleagues and students never understood or appreciated my unique experiences on the reservation. They only created a distance of inquiry about my identity as an Indian.

I allowed myself to become a simulation on the good road of my personal experience, and now the time has come to abandon that passive fakery and become a new postindian on a much better road. My roads have always been better than your roads. You cornered me for a time on your mundane roads.

Listen, why not come with me tonight?

☞ 9 ☜

Postindian Holograms

Almost Browne, who was almost born on the reservation, inspired a generation of native newcomers with marvelous laser projections of shamans, warriors, politicians, federal agents, and totemic animals and birds in three dimensions. He was renowned for the creation of ethereal holographic laser portrayals of natives, animals, and birds on more than a hundred reservations, and over parks, docks, athletic fields, meadows, forests, rivers, and estates in major cities around the country.

Almost was named a feral laser trickster.

Since his banishment the trickster has been a laser migrant, and so he was eager to accept an invitation from my cousin and the native students on campus to teach seminars on the creative art of laser holograms and historical portrayals in the Department of Native American Indian Studies.

Almost was the first and only native to be banished from his family home and reservation for the creation of laser holograms and eccentric portrayals. The laser projections were weak overhead, a mere shimmer of greenish light, and yet the images unnerved the terminal believers, and rivaled the aurora borealis and the Milky Way. He projected the distorted faces of reservation politicians at laser wakes over the water tower. The politicians rebuked the laser troublemaker.

Federal agents were portrayed as laser vultures hovering over the outhouses, and one by one he teased the missionaries with laser images of the crucifix. Jesus Christ was laser nailed to the cross by the wrists, not by the hands. The hidebound tribal judge ruled that the laser shaman was not a traditional guiding light and banished him forever from the White Earth Reservation.

Almost had projected on the night of a new moon a giant laser holographic visage of Christopher Columbus rising slowly over the white pine, mission pond, and reservation cemetery. That unsteady image, the mere ironic shimmer of the ghostly explorer, amused some citizens and haunted others on the reservation. The public health nurse worried about epidemics. The shamanic possession of that shimmer of laser beams at night worried the priests and nuns at the Mission of Saint Benedict.

Columbus was pale, greenish, gauzy, irrelevant, and ironic, and yet the mere trace and shimmer of that stray aerial explorer provoked the priest to denounce the demonic creatures of the night sky, and to remonstrate with the judge to order the removal and banishment of the laser artist that summer from the reservation.

Columbus was a trace of fury.

The trickster moved to the city and projected laser images of native warriors and huge animals over the interstates. He created the laser images of white men on the reservation, and laser holograms of natives and animals over the interstates in the city.

Almost was seldom interested in stunners, ideologies, politics, or theories, but for those that had marvelous aspects and dimensions. He was inspired as a child by the ironic teases and evasive stories of shamans, the motion of tricksters, and stray visions. Yes, he used that expression, "stray visions." Native shamans and tricksters were storiers of stray visions. Almost was inspired by feral images, the features and renditions of native memories and stories. The creation of laser holograms and portrayals was a sublime practice, but not, of course, at the wake of irony on a reservation where the politicians masqueraded with extreme feigns, and at the same time emulated native traditions.

The holographic native warriors and feral animals that the trickster projected with laser beams over urban lakes, parks, and interstate highways were natural amusement, an aesthetic reminder of the native world at night. Almost was praised for his contribution to the enrichment of the community, but that sentiment turned sour when the laser trickster created a bear and three greenish moose over a rise and curve on the interstate. The bear wandered onto the median, turned, shivered, and then vanished. That night the traffic was backed up for more than three miles. The police received hundreds of emergency reports about the strange migration of dangerous animals on the interstate highway.

Almost was plainly pleased to have the invitation, and for more than the obvious reasons, to teach at the university. He had become a fugitive from justice for laser abuses of the night, an uncertain allegation of criminal activity. The police in several cities had seized the lasers and he was cited by state and federal prosecutors for domestic terrorism, the cause of public panic and disturbance, endangerment of humans on an interstate, the mistreatment of feral animals, and the practice of entertainment without a proper license.

Almost was prosecuted as a laser criminal.

Almost told the state judge at the hearing that lasers heal in three dimensions, and natives have inherent rights to hunt animals by laser, gun, or bow and arrow, and in any season. He explained that the historical figures he portrayed by laser beams over the interstates had been already simulated on cereal boxes, balloons, advertisements, and paper money. Almost insisted that cities come alive, a virtual ecstasy with laser holograms at night. The laser portrayals of warriors, presidents, and feral animals have the right to come together by laser light at night.

The Minneapolis Tribune reported that Barry Croisade, the state district judge, ruled in favor of the native laser artist and his overnight characters, including Crazy Horse, Sitting Bull, Chief Joseph, Geronimo, Jim Thorpe, George Armstrong Custer, Harry Truman, Richard Nixon, Christopher Columbus, bears, wolves, moose, sandhill cranes, and other feral laser birds and animals.

Crazy Horse was a visage only conceived, of course, because there were no images or photographs of the great warrior. Natives and others described him as an ecstatic visionary, and he endures by that account with Jesus Christ. The judge was inspired by the laser artist and pronounced that the "laser is a native pen, a light brush in the wild night, and the laser warriors are new creations, an instance of native communal rights, continental liberty, and without a nightly doubt free expression under the First Amendment of the United States Constitution."

Captain Shammer printed that judicial decision and mounted the document near the door of Postindian Holograms. Almost and the students in the first seminar of laser arts worked at night, but even by day shimmers of blue and green light were revealed under the door of the former faculty office. No one, not even the dean, dared to enter the laser sanctum without an invitation for fear of crashing an ethereal figure.

Justice Miles Lord should have heard the case of terrorism and laser crimes against the peace in federal court, but he was presiding over another case of native liberty. Justice Marion Troubadour, an exotic name from the fur trade, presided in federal court and ruled in favor of the laser artist as a native with ancient rights to create or hunt at night. The laser holograph characters are evidence of native creative and ironic expressions, not acts of terror in the night.

Almost was banished once and twice acquitted.

Justices Lord, Troubadour, and Croisade were projected over the university walk bridge for several nights, the first laser holograms created by students in the seminar on Postindian Holograms. The dean assured the senior faculty that the campus was not under judicial or military laser scrutiny. Slash and Burn told a newspaper reporter that one night the entire faculty and administration might be represented in laser flight over the campus.

John Berryman was projected a few nights later over the same bridge, a haunting and ghostly laser image of the poet and professor who leaped to his death. The senior faculty was not pleased by the portrayal, a desecration of the great poet, and tried to censure the students in the laser seminar.

Almost had obtained the necessary photographs and motion picture images of the very professors who favored the censure of laser art on campus. The laser students projected each of their faces over the university boathouse. On the third night as the shimmer of faces dissolved one into the other near the river the dean announced without delay his absolute support for the free expression of laser art on the campus. Naturally, the next night the mighty laser image of the dean was projected in jerky flight over the law school.

Captain Shammer had overturned the nasty manners and dissolution of the senior faculty in the department by the second semester. The once loathsome tenured faculty, removed from their private offices, now celebrated the chairman for his incredible academic entrepreneurial adventures. My cousin created new enterprises that increased student enrollment, and raised thousands of dollars in user fees, endorsements, subscriptions, and laser contracts. Native studies reported a significant financial gain in the very first semester, the only department at the university with cash reserves from native ventures, and not from covert research or federal grants.

Slash and Burn beamed at the monetary news and never failed to mention his solemn duty to protect the sacred birch tree in his office, a natural association with natives and new revenue, and he used the same mundane metaphor to express his respect and praise of the onetime untutored houseboat captain who had initiated the spectacular centers of panic, irony, last lectures, trickster commerce, laser holograms, and the native denivance publishers.

Almost and the students in the seminar created four laser portrayals of rich entrepreneurs and investors and projected their images in three dimensions over the corporate headquarters of Honeywell, 3M Company, Cargill, General Mills, and the English Department at the University of Minnesota to honor the native enterpriser and speculator Captain Shammer from Lake Itasca and the ancient headwaters of the Mississippi River.

Andrew Carnegie as a laser hologram financier in flight over the headquarters of Honeywell was an obvious tease of capitalism, but the projection of rich white men at night over the

Department of English was truly a mystery. Almost explained that literary artists and the captains of literature have changed more in the world than any industrialist or media magnate. One creative literary image has more sway in stories and memory than a parfleche of money. Carnegie funded many libraries but the books on the shelves await creative readers. Thomas Wolfe, Willa Cather, D'Arcy McNickle, Mark Twain, and their novels are more memorable than the cash flow of philanthropists.

The four laser robber barons, John Jacob Astor, John Pierpont Morgan, John D. Rockefeller, and Carnegie, were projected over the nerve centers of vast corporations in the city. John Jacob Astor the furrier and real estate financier wore laser beaver and, of course, a greenish turkey feather bonnet. John Pierpont Morgan the financier and generous art collector wobbled that night with an eerie distended nose. He had sponsored the romantic production and publication of aesthetic photographs of natives by Edward Sheriff Curtis. John D. Rockefeller the oil and railroad industrialist was a pioneer in the support of medical research, and a generous contributor to education. His moustache was huge, greenish over the corporate gardens of General Mills. Rockefeller waved a banner with the name of the University of Chicago. The seminar students could not account for the ghostly laser bounce and scatter that night of Andrew Carnegie.

Hole in the Day, an eminent native visionary and warrior, was projected in three dimensions over Fort Snelling, an early nineteenth century military post near the great confluence of the Minnesota and Mississippi Rivers. The laser hologram of Hole in the Day with his Winchester rifle was considered a radical native presence by the state governor, no matter the practice and protection of laser art at the university.

Federal agents had arrested Hole in the Day and other warriors at Onigum on the Leech Lake Reservation. They were charged with trivial offenses, refusing to testify in court about the white men who smuggled and sold alcohol to natives. Hole in the Day, a healer who lived at Sugar Point near Bear Island on Leech Lake, escaped that afternoon. The federal agents were shamed and cried wolf to cover their mistake. That deceptive cry incited a war between natives and the United States Army.

Hole in the Day roamed night after night as a laser warrior over Fort Snelling. Almost and the students strategically positioned the laser beams within the federal border of the old fort, on former government property. The land at the confluence of the rivers had been stolen from the Anishinaabe and Dakota to establish a military presence in the territory.

Almost projected a great laser warrior over the fort to provoke the state and federal government to return the land to natives. The laser war at the old fort inspired feature stories in newspapers about the early military presence at Fort Snelling, and about Hole in the Day and the war at Sugar Point on the Leech Lake Reservation.

Hole in the Day was an elusive warrior who had lived in a cabin at Sugar Point. Soldiers invaded the point, occupied his cabin, stole his sacred ceremonial vestments, and trampled the vegetables in his gardens. The Pillager warriors, outnumbered more than three to one, routed the immigrant soldiers on a single day in October 1898. There were no reports of native casualties, but the army lost six dead and eleven wounded, a singular defeat of the Third Infantry.

Almost dared his seminar students to create a laser animation of selected scenes from native ledger art. The untutored native artists and political prisoners at Fort Marion in Saint Augustine, Florida, drew ceremonies and many horses with colored pencils.

The visionary drawings were sold to tourists at the time, and were collected later by individuals and museums. The students were inspired with the native artists, already modernist, or cosmoprimitive by the style and composition of scenes with colored pencils. The many horses were visionary, drawn in many colors, blue horses, red horses, and yellow horses. The horses were in sublime motion with no vanishing point, and were not mere representations of realism or naturalism.

The students created laser horses drawn by the prison artists Zotom, Making Medicine, Squint Eyes, White Bear, and Howling Wolf. They waited for the new moon, a warm, clear night to project the laser ledger art horses over the Armory Gardens near the Guthrie Theater and Walker Art Center. The students projected several laser horses at the same time, the visionary motion of horses on the plains. There was no public announcement, but word of the laser show passed from person to person and hundreds of people gathered on the grass to watch the marvelous motion of native visionary horses.

Almost and the students presented the laser horses on three consecutive nights, and each night the audience increased by the hundreds. Many people arrived at sunset, and yet the spectators never knew if a laser projection was actually scheduled. The students had become native masters of the laser arts. On the last night the visionary laser horses moved in circles one last time over the Armory Gardens and then together the horses galloped toward the west and the plains. The audience waited in silence, searching the night sky for the horses, and then broke into applause for the laser artists.

Making Medicine was riding a blue horse.

The last laser portrayal was in motion over the giant elm trees as the audience continued to applaud the spectacular projection of ledger art horses. The laser portrayal was of Richard Henry Pratt, a lieutenant in the army at the time, who encouraged native prisoners to assimilate as educated artists, and who later founded the first native boarding school not located on a reservation, the Carlisle Indian Industrial School.

Suddenly the enthusiasm of the audience turned to silence as the laser lieutenant moved closer to the Armory Gardens on his military horse. Several men, apparently veterans, saluted the lieutenant. Others in the audience pointed and shouted at the laser scene of a uniformed army officer riding in the night sky. Lieutenant Pratt slowly turned toward the spectators in the sculpture garden, a laser episode of realism, and returned the salute. The laser lieutenant lurched on his horse, shimmered, and then vanished over the Walker Art Center.

🖝 10 🖜

Denivance Press

Roberta Lee Royalty established a grandiose media empire that only pretends to publish books by distinguished authors. She named the curious enterprise the Denivance Press. The publisher, a former overseer of the celebrated Two Spirit Séance Salons, traced her native ancestors to a mysterious culture in the West Indies, and to the mighty Confederate general, Robert Edward Lee, of the United States Civil War.

Lee Royalty named her Bichon Frisé Appomattox.

The Denivance Press was first named the Renunciation Book Company, but Lee Royalty converted the numbers and a single letter of the alphabet into an original name for a company that refuses, and with panache, to consider any original manuscripts for publication. The absolute denial of manuscripts from the best and the brightest authors was the ironic maxim of the press.

Captain Shammer was impressed, of course, with the maxim, a publisher that denies the best manuscripts by earnest authors, and invited her to move the operation of the press into a faculty office in the department. Lee Royalty had denied many native authors from the corner of her bedroom, but now the mighty denials were rightly associated with native studies and the university.

Captain Shammer encouraged the faculty and students to tease the founder and the name of the press. My cousin was more like our grandfather, Captain Eighty, because he was a storier not a reader, and he took more pleasure in the sound than the silence of printed words. Quiver, our grandmother, was the reader on the houseboat, and she inspired me to discover a sense of liberty in every word and sentence of a book.

Mere titles were for the literary tease and irony, not the liberty. So, the enthusiasm of my cousin for the publication of blank books, a later enterprise, was not only the absence of printed words. The Denivance Press was a source of absolute irony, and that incredible literary gesture might have turned him into a reader.

Denivance was a contrived and clever word that earned some respect in the lexicon of publishers. Captain Shammer chanted words of resistance and ironic variations of the name—denivance, deny, thumbs down, repudiate, refuse, contradict, counter, decline, rebuff, eschew, renounce, and take a chance—to gainsay.

Lee Royalty told my cousin that she started with the words deny and denial, and then connected the letter "vee" with the suffix that denoted action, and created the word denivance. She was quick to explain, however, that there was more to the name of the press than the mere vee and a state of action. The letter vee in denivance was the twenty-second letter of the alphabet, a natural number. So, she declared, there are twenty-two chapters of the Revelation of John, the number of players on the field in football, the length of a cricket pitch, the novel *Catch-22* by

Joseph Heller, and, of course, the natural number of a Psalm in The Old Testament. *My God, my God, why have you forsaken me? Why are you so far from saving me, so far from heeding my groans?* The Denivance Press had forsaken many authors, and at the same time saved them from the eternal shame of publication. Lee Royalty teased the faculty that no sincere author can bear to read his own book after a few years. So, she reasoned, why not treasure a denial and avoid the shame? She was cheeky and tried to solicit the most significant native authors and the best academic manuscripts for rejection by Denivance Press. A prompt denial letter was an ironic measure of the very highest standards of native erudition and academic achievement.

Formal denial letters from Denivance Press were cited in new academic appointments, reviews, and many promotions. Professor Abraham Pump, for instance, an expert on new ethnic victimry, was promoted with tenure not for the count of his actual publications, or the number of unpublished manuscripts, but because he had earned three concise letters of absolute denial from the Denivance Press.

Lee Royalty wrote the concise letters of denial. Each letter of denial was formal and original, and with discrete comments on the outstanding research and literary style of the rejected manu-scripts. These letters have become precious collectables. Decades later, after my cousin vanished, and the incredible auction of the department, the press continued the signature tradition of ironic denials of manuscripts by native authors. The Denivance Press had become a respected and historical institution at the university.

Several native authors complained constantly and refused to accept a denial from the Denivance Press. They persisted month after month and were determined to become published authors. These double denials of native authors inspired the editors to concoct a new and very successful editorial division of Denivance Press.

Captain Shammer and Roberta Lee Royalty initiated a signature edition, a new series of hardbound academic blank books. The Livre Blanc series considered the publication of significant titles, and only titles. The Livre Blanc series of books were blank, absolutely blank, but each edition was published with tinted laid paper, deckle edge, and signature bound in the tradition of fine octavo book production. The blank books were aesthetic, and had absolutely no content to distract the reader.

There were several notable blank book publishers at the time, but only one teased the actual titles of books by famous authors. Franz Montgomery, professor emeritus, and memorable poker loser at the Full House Casino, was a fancier of blank books by famous authors, such as *The Grapes of Wrath* by John Steinbeck, *The Deerslayer*, by James Fenimore Cooper, *Elmer Gantry* by Sinclair Lewis, and *War and Peace* by Leo Tolstoy.

Quiver, my grandmother, once asked the literature professor at a poker game to sign and dedicate two copies of his blank books for her grandsons Dogroy and Captain Shammer. The professor denied the request, even after my grandmother bought new blank copies of *The Last of the Mohicans*, and *House Made of Dawn*. The Livre Blanc series published only original and ironic titles, not the mere titles of previously published books. So, there was never any serious competition of blank book publishers.

Almost Browne was actually the first blank book publisher on the reservation and in the state. Wigwass Trade Books, a series of blank books with distinctive calico cloth covers, were best sellers at the university. Almost and his family bound the books by hand on the reservation. He sold the books from the back of a station wagon in a loading zone at the university.

The signature blank books were published with familiar titles, and only titles, such as *The Hungry Generation* by D'Arcy McNickle, *The Way to Rainy Mountain* by N. Scott Momaday, *Ceremony* by Leslie Silko, and *The Everlasting Sky* by Gerald Vizenor. Almost signed and inscribed each of the blank books in the name of the author. Several times, however, he signed copies of *Talking to the Moon* by John Joseph Mathews as John Steinbeck, and boldly signed *Look Homeward Angel* by Thomas Wolfe in the name of Luther Standing Bear.

Almost also signed and inscribed books in the name of Jesus Christ, Vine Deloria, Crazy Horse, Geoffrey Chaucer, and William Shakespeare. Many book buyers were curious about the native publisher from the reservation. Where did he learn how to read, write, and publish books? Almost told his loyal customers at the university that he learned how to read on his own, from books that had been burned in a fire at the Nibwaakaa Library on the White Earth Reservation. The few books rescued from the ashes were burned on the sides and the corners. Almost saved copies of burned books and learned to read from the centers of the books, and then he imagined stories from the absence of words, from the words that had burned in the fire.

Natives envision the burned words.

Franz Montgomery, the literature professor, and later the testy poker loser, was one of his most enthusiastic customers, and bought a copy of every edition published by Wigwass Trade Books. Almost was arrested by university police for consumer fraud and conducting a commercial business on state property without a license. Professor Montgomery, who was known at the time as Monte Franzgomery, told the judge at the hearing that the accused was a native publisher and had natural treaty rights to conduct business on the campus of a land grant university.

The professor testified that the faculty and students were the trespassers, not the natives, because the land had been stolen from natives. Moreover, the professor told the judge that blank books made more sense to him than anything he had read in the past decade at the university. Montgomery exaggerated the case, and his testimony was unreliable, but the professor always required his students to buy Wigwass Trade Books.

Denivance Press published blank books in the same tradition but with the titles, and only titles, of native dream songs, and later published the blank book titles of literature by native and other authors. The early native dream song titles were very distinctive publications, and were bound in simulated birch bark. The titles were dream songs about bears, bear paths, love, charms, owl medicine, flying feathers, loons, dance, and these titles: *Come, let us drink*; *I am as brave as other men*; *Do not weep*; *My love has departed*; *My music reaches to the sky*; *My voice is heard*; and *I go to the big bear's lodge*.

Elizabeth Cook-Lynn steadfastly refused to even consider the signature invitation to have one of her manuscripts denied for publication. Lee Royalty was mighty persuasive at a prairie séance a decade later but she could not overcome the wrath and refusal of the cranky author.

The inaugural publication of the new series was celebrated in the communal faculty offices of the department. The scent of cedar and the steady, rapid beat of hand drums created the sense of a native ceremony and sanctuary. The native faculty authors were no strangers to book parties. The faculty authors appreciated the blank book irony but they were hesitant to embrace the notion of manuscript denials, however concise, for merit promotions.

Suddenly the drums were silent. Lee Royalty removed the blue velvet that covered the first precious publication of the Livre

Blanc series by Denivance Press. She raised the book over her head for everyone to see, and then she shouted out the catchy title, almost as a warning, *Why I Can't Read Elizabeth Cook-Lynn and Other Essays: A Voice from the Dead* by Wallace Stegner.

The faculty turned in silence, and then an incredulous native student raised her hands and waved, a gesture to deny the obvious irony, but the other graduate students burst into laughter and overcame the untimely grievance about the tricky title. Actually, no one was certain about the meaning of the title.

The University of Wisconsin Press had published *Why I Can't Read Wallace Stegner and Other Essays: A Tribal Voice*, a biased diatribe by Elizabeth Cook-Lynn. Lee Royalty easily turned that title around to present the crotchety author as a hard and negative read. Madeline Seams, the former graduate student later appointed as a professor in the department, announced that the original title by Cook-Lynn was ambiguous. Apparently the other essays in the book are also hard to read, not only Wallace Stegner. So, that title was a natural invitation to publish the ironic title of a blank book by the deceased author. Cook-Lynn apparently had not closely read any books by Wallace Stegner.

The Livre Blanc series published six titles of blank books that semester, and each publication was a celebration by the faculty and students. Slash and Burn, who was close to retirement, attended every blank book event because the proceeds from the sale of original titles by Livre Blanc and Denivance Press were second only to the income from the losers at the Full House Casino. Clearly more copies of blank books with ironic titles were purchased on campus than ordinary books with original content.

Lee Royalty was invited to consult with other departments about the blank book enterprise and Denivance Press. She presented copies of the ironic blank books to the deans and to selected chairmen of other departments. Sociology, political science, education, and economics, to name only four, were mainstream departments with a noticeable absence of irony, so there was no reason to present copies of the ironic titles of blank books.

The Livre Blanc edition of *Why I Can't Read Elizabeth Cook-Lynn and Other Essays: A Voice from the Dead* by Wallace Stegner was a best seller. The blank title actually received a very positive review in a local newspaper. The reviewer commented on the irony of the popularity of blank books on the campus. Lee Royalty and the student editors were featured as the postindian transformers of the native studies department, the steady mockers of the university, and ironic founders of the Denivance Press.

The incredible publication success of the title *Why I Can't Read Elizabeth Cook-Lynn and Other Essays* prompted the immediate publication of an associated ironic blank book title, *Who's Afraid of Elizabeth Cook-Lynn?* by Robert Breast Brave. The ironic title was obviously inspired by the play *Who's Afraid of Virginia Woolf?* by Edward Albee.

Other ironic blank book titles published in the Livre Blanc series included the sensational *Four American Indian Literary Masturbators* by Alan Velie; the *Rhymists of Blank Verse* by Jim Barnes; the rebirth of *The Crown of Columbus* as the *Dick of Columbus* by Harry Handler; the revised title of a famous novel by William Faulkner, *Noise and the Fury* by Bucky Porter; the ironic teaser, *Native Wind in the Willows: An Anthology of Literary Sniffs and Whiffs* by Almost Robert Lee; the conversion of *Understanding Gerald Vizenor* into the ironic double negative title, *No One Can Not Understand Gerald Vizenor*, by Deborah Madsen; and the most recent blank book title teaser, *Go Tell It on the Prairie Not the Mountain: Brave Buffalo Soldiers of the Tenth Cavalry Regiment*, by Valmont Premier.

🖝 11 🖜

Stray Visions

Captain Shammer was praised as a storier of natural reason and survivance, and yet he resisted any discussion of the definition or meaning of his creative practices. The faculty appreciated the humane and ironic manner of the houseboat storier and academic entrepreneur but they could not clearly understand the notion of natural reason and stray visions.

My cousin was evasive and never revealed to strangers any connotations of native sentiments. Shammer carried out the actual stories of survivance, but not the arbitrary or common conversations of survivance. He was cagey and seldom responded to doubts and queries because academics revise and consume ideas rather than create stories. Natural reason, stray visions, and survivance were creative maneuvers, not academic conversations.

Shammer recounted a new native consciousness. He was inspired by our grandfather who was an exceptional native storier. My cousin learned how to perceive the union of chance and nature, and then to create intuitive stories about native coincidence, but he was always disheartened by excuses, and pestered by interpretations and mere definitions. Stray visions were always teachable by irony, by incongruity, and by the play of contradictions, but not by deadbolt structural interpretations, the definitions of culture by anthropology, or the representations of absence in history.

Shammer was rightly equivocal about natural reason.

That marvelous sense of chance, presence, and motion of the seasons was the sublime source of stray visions, natural reason, and trickster consciousness. My cousin learned how to counter natural and simulated misery, and how to outmaneuver the coercion of federal agents and the daily traders of political sleaze and cultural extortion. He counteracted the history of native absence and victimry by stray visions, irony, and native stories of survivance.

Quiver teased the losers and maintained the faculty poker and student moccasin games at the casino, but she continued to worry, and for good reason, that her grandson was uneasy, even bored, by the end of the second semester, with the creative academic centers that he had inaugurated in the department. My cousin was truly inspired by the stories of panic holes, last lectures, irony dogs, holograms, by the ironic denial of manuscripts, and the publication of sensational blank books by Denivance Press. The ironic titles were closer to stories, a natural tease, and faraway from printed words, but day by day he become more distracted by the wearisome assessments, evaluations, tedious revisions, vacuous academic considerations, and administrative aesthetics of his native enterprises at the university.

Captain Shammer saluted chance and untamed native visions, the very practices of our grandfather. Captain Eighty and my cousin were houseboat visionaries. They perceived the chance of motion, break of day, turn of waves, eternal migration of cranes, cardinals, escorts of monarch butterflies, thunderstorms, ravens at the headwaters.

The shoreline creatures were never the same by seasons.

My grandfather and cousin were captains of a houseboat, and likewise the captain of any enterprise must have the wit to perceive chance and natural reason, and to create ironic stories.

My cousin was distracted with simulations and the aesthetics of native studies, so he diverted the mundane by irony and created a new estate of natural reason and stories of action, the exotic stray visions of the Eighty Estate. The new estate of native liberty honored our grandfather Captain Eighty.

Captain Eighty was the inspiration of the Eighty Estate.

The first four estates of dominance, clergy, nobility, ordinary citizens, and the media have simulated natives as cultural separatists, savages, animists, innate ecologists, and many, many other peculiar concoctions by the sentiments of estate victimry. Everyone knows that natives were swindled and betrayed by four, five, and even six crucial estates of nationalism. These estates were desperate, already at the very ruins of monotheism and civilization, and the estates never represented native imagination or continental liberty.

The native premise of postindian overturns the most obvious cultural simulations. The theory of the postindian escapes the need for upper case letters, and leaves the remains of cultural invention to the nostalgia of the four estates of dominance.

The Eighty Estate was stories of stray visions.

The dandelions were always the first to bloom at the end of winter, and the first bright rosettes attracted eager insects, birds, and children in the parks. My cousin was enticed by the turn of seasons, the migration road songs of the cardinals, the majestic tours of great sandhill cranes, noisy beavers at the headwaters, bold sumac at every natural crease, meadowlarks on the wire, the slight shadows at twilight, traces of blossoms, willow catkins, and the natural reason of these images and stray visions. The faculty never mentioned these natural associations in more than possessive pronouns of separation.

Captain Shammer vanished for a few days in the spring. That was not the first time he vanished during the academic year, but his hasty exits had become more frequent. He returned, several days later, from a grove of aromatic cedar in the heart of the Chippewa Nation Forest. He came back with a proposal for a course on natural reason, survivance, native irony, and stray visions. My cousin created the marvelous native centers and invited many extraordinary storiers and teachers, but he had never prepared or taught a course in the department.

Shammer was a teaser and evasive teacher.

The Livre Blanc series published a special deckle edge edition of *Stray Visions* by Captain Shammer. This was his first blank book title for use in the seminar on stray visions. My cousin was a storier, not a reader, so he had resisted teaching because he did not want to read, but for the new seminar he required only one blank book for the entire semester. Naturally, the classroom was very crowded on the first day. The students were standing in the aisles of the room, but only seven graduate students remained after my cousin described the practices of the seminar. Nothing could be more daunting to most students than to pack a blank book with original ideas about natural reason and stray visions. The notion of stray visions chased away most of the academic consumers. The students who remained were curious, anxious, and dedicated to the subject of natural reason, and they would learn to perceive stray visions.

Captain Shaman invited the students to practice natural reason, to search for stray visions in the least likely places, but not in libraries, and to consider original ideas, visual scenes, and to create ironic stories. He required the students to live by stray visions and imagination on the street, under bridges, and to become vagrants overnight in the junkyards on the river-bank near the university. Or, he teased, wear a celebrity mask and encounter ordinary scenes and situations in the city. Walk through the airport wearing a mask of John Wayne, bear witness at a rescue mission, loiter in expensive restaurants in the mask of Mother Teresa, wear a clerical miter and buy a deadbolt at a hardware store, exercise with the Reserve Officers' Training Corps in the athletic facility at the university in the mask of Geronimo, and then create stories about the responses to the mask. The students were obligated to create and write down the necessary perceptions and original stories in the crucial blank book, *Stray Visions*.

Shammer warned that at the end of the semester every blank page in *Stray Visions* must be covered with notes, statements, literary perceptions, imagistic poems, original stories about natural reason and survivance, and the students must practice as storiers in the seminar. He meant that each student must contest historical representations of absence and create a sense of presence in a story, and other students would continue the same story with original scenes of natural reason and stray visions. He explained, for instance, that a story about hungry children housed in cardboard boxes under a bridge would be continued by other students in the seminar, stories about ravens that carried the box of children to the rotunda of the state capital, or other stories about the migration and magical flight of children. My cousin encouraged ironic stories about native houseboat captains, the songs and teases of moccasin games, visions, dreams, and thunderstorms late at night. Shammer coaxed and teased the students to run with the irony dogs and discover a continent of liberty.

Captain Shammer created stories about the natural motion of animals and birds, the shadows, gestures, and perception of totemic associations. Walk with a raven, he told the students, and he mocked the walk of a raven, and then he lowered his head and moved with a bear. He encouraged the students to imagine and imitate the natural motion of animals and birds. He explained that every natural motion and shadow is a stray vision. Later he moved across the seminar room in the gentle manner and sway of a great sandhill crane. Swim with a river otter, and my cousin treaded water at the surface of the seminar chairs. His eyes were watery. The motion of his body and facial expressions entranced the students.

My cousin created a nickname for each of the seven native graduate students, Night Light, Highbrow, Double Negative, Holy Grail, Promissory, General Badger, and Trauma Queen. Only three of the native students had previous nicknames. The tease of nicknames was an essential introduction to native irony and survivance. Nicknames were survivance stories because the necessary tease is communal, a gesture of association and acceptance. Totemic associations are the natural tease of animals and birds. Naturally, some of the students were hesitant, shied by the attention of new ironic nicknames.

Night Light was a roamer who wore socks with bright stripes and polka dots. She earned the nickname by the bright colors of the socks, but otherwise she was a reserved Cherokee Freedmen. The metaphors of color and the nasty politics of race affected the way she expressed her experiences.

Night Light created stories about rats and cardboard in her blank book of stray visions. She discovered that the sound of the stories in the seminar sessions were not the same as what she had written in *Stray Visions*. Some of the scenes changed by the tone of voice, by the visual traces of light and creation. And, other students focused on aspects of the experience she had not considered in her stories.

The scent of cardboard, wet cardboard, is always with me, here and in my dreams, and in every trace of memory. That scent is my sense of a stray vision, and so is my connection with sewer rats under the university walk bridge. The rats give off the same scent of wet cardboard, and now the rats know me by a mere whiff of my body. The rats are with me at night, and we are more secure together than in the day light gaze of racists and tribal politicians. The rats have become my night family. Yes, we live in the cardboard under the bridge, truly a stray vision and totemic association that was never possible with those wicked separatists of the Cherokee Nation.

Highbrow was Lumbee with a distinctive accent from North Carolina. He wore starched button down shirts, floral ties, and an expensive sport coat. He was obviously more conservative than the other students in the seminar, so he decided to pursue a stray vision as a proper liberal politician. Highbrow wore a mask of Hubert Humphrey, the former senator and vice president, and loitered in bank lobbies, attended an adult movie theater, and tried to meet the president of Cargill, the private multinational corporation located in Minnetonka, near Minneapolis, Minnesota.

I am not accustomed to loitering, and certainly have never sought a stray vision, or any vision for that matter, but the mask provided me with a very comfortable disguise in public. I was rather at peace in a mask, and was not obligated to maintain my own character or identity. In other words, the mask was something of a stray vision because it made it possible for me to experience a sense of liberty.

Bank lobbies would never, in my estimation, be a place to find a stray vision, much less a place to create a story. Bank visions are hardly strays. I was mistaken, however, about the stories. There are many potential stories about that masked man in the bank lobby.

Lingering in the lobby of a downtown bank, not an ordinary experience for me, would have caused me great embarrassment, but for the political disguise of the mask. Customers could not avoid the resemblance of the distinguished politician, but the responses were not predictable in any sense. Some customers were moved by the simulated visage of Hubert Humphrey. Others were doubtful and eyed my height, as the vice president was much shorted and stouter than me. The delayed responses were the most dynamic, and some were very troubling. Several good citizens broke into tears at the mere mask of Humphrey. I was actually moved by the expressions of emotion, but then three customers shouted at me in the lobby. One burly man threatened me physically, pushed me away from the customer counter, punched me in the chest, and cursed me for making fun of one of the greatest politicians in America. He tore the mask from my face, and shouted at me that I did not deserve to be a citizen of the country if I made fun of Hubert Humphrey.

The pleasure of my disguise was completely reversed, and instead it became a great burden. I was massively embarrassed and attempted to apologize for my behavior. I explained that the mask was only a graduate seminar assignment to pursue a stray vision. That comment, of course, did not impress anyone, not even me. The man who pushed me was in a rage, his breath was much too rapid, and he leaned on the counter. The customers had backed away, and avoided the entire scene. Finally a bank security guard asked me what had happened, and about the nature of the mask.

I told the guard and a bank official that my respect for the great

Hubert Humphrey was so intense that from time to time I wear a mask to be closer to the liberal principals he represented as an elected official and promoted as a legislator. My vision of the vice president was more intimate and heartfelt in a mask of his likeness. Truly, this was a profound encounter for me, to experience the strong emotions of so many people who identify with the dignity and humanity of Hubert Humphrey.

My vision and vicarious experience of the vice president has brought me closer to a liberal consciousness and political philosophy than any history, personal testimony, party platform, or legislative documents. Who would have thought that a heartfelt liberal sentiment would have come to me as a seminar obligation to pursue a stray and emotive vision in a mask?

I would rather not describe my masked experiences at the adult movie theater, except to say that on that evening the Faust Theater in Saint Paul presented the popular pornographic film, Behind the Green Door, *starring Marilyn Chambers. A woman in the audience shouted,* Oh no, not in the ass again! *No one seemed to noticed the man in the theater who wore the mask of Hubert Humphrey.*

Double Negative was Dakota, and she declared that no one would not want to be native. She perceived most associations and situations in double negatives, stories and comments that seemed to reveal the positive. Double Negative convinced my cousin that the evasive manner of double negatives was a practice of survivance, a strategic literary dodge of native absence and victimry. The positive sense of double negative comments is tricky, cumbersome, and deceptive, but the outcome is survivance, and a trace of stray visions.

I went to the historical society museum and not for nothing natives were contained in rooms and enclaves as exhibition subjects, and always with no sense of absence. I don't know nothing but natives are a presence. I am a presence, not a nobody in the museum. I didn't say nothing at first, but the docents were so pleasant, so happy, smiley, and eager to never say a nasty word. I would never not want to shout "no shit" and "no, no fuck" over dinner in honor of the presence of natives at a museum. The docents were trained to talk in double positives, and that only came out as a negative. So sorry, so kind. Yes, yes, yes, you are so right. No, no, no, the docents were wrong. Most of my friends never think not to make a negative out of two positives, but a really smart instructor at the university teased my double negatives with his double positives. You never understand, you don't got no sense about the negative of double positives. Yeah, right, so you talk. I am not, not a negative person. Yeah, same difference, so you talk again. I just can't get no satisfaction talking in double positives.

Natives don't never need no museum, no, no, we are museums in motion. Yes, yes, you are so kind to comment on the history of the state historical museum. Now, that talk never would not end, not even, yeah, right, in stray visions.

Holy Grail was Métis Cree from Winnipeg, Manitoba, Canada. He was already a fur trade storier and songster, more by academic adventures than by irony and survivance. Holy Grail carried a metal camping cup attached to his belt, clank, clank, clank down the hallway.

Holy was inspired by native evangelism, and dedicated to combine the way of life of a roamer preacher with the stories, music, and sentiments of the fur trade. Never mind, he assured the other students in the seminar, that the fur trade was imagined, an aesthetic trade because he could never sacrifice an animal. He was teased and nicknamed a postindian fur trader by the students.

Holy was determined to convert the traditional vision quest for a guardian spirit into a secular search for stray visions and, naturally, for a high final grade in the seminar. He declared that his pursuit of a vision would never harm any form of life. His vision would be pure, ethical, and never tainted by sacrifice. That was near the end of the graduate semester. Later he encountered the wicked mosquitoes in the boundary waters of Ontario and Minnesota.

I packed my tent, drove to the Boundary Waters Canoe Area, and rented a canoe at a resort on Gunflint Lake in the Superior National Forest. I paddled for a day and camped on an island with a view of the west. The island had to be just right, with a giant rock near the shore where I could meditate and watch the sun set over the lake. I saw only two other canoes at a distance, and never heard a sound of humans for three days. The weather was perfect, only a slight breeze, and the loons were elusive.

I pitched my tent, ate an early camp dinner, and waited on the rock for the sun to set. The sun glanced over the water, and shivered with the breeze. I was in paradise on that ancient granite rock, and prepared to experience a mighty vision. Nothing could distract me. Not a human in sight. The loons started to sing, and the echo and response of other loons was a haunting sound on the lake. I wanted to sing the same songs, to break my separation from nature. The sun moved lower, and the air was slightly chilled. I was totally relaxed, actually in a state of meditation. As the sun shimmered over the lake and behind the distant trees, the breeze suddenly ended as the sun set, and then the mosquitoes arrived in huge swarms. I was not prepared for those tiny mosquitoes, desperate to taste the blood of the first camper of the season. I covered my head with a sweatshirt, and tried to chase the mosquitoes away from my hands, but they were noisy and determined to have my blood that night.

The sky was magnificent, a few thin clouds and greats streaks and sweeps of color, rose, bluish, spring green over the trees. This was my moment to be at peace with an eternal vision of nature. The buzz and hum of thousands of mosquitoes around my head and hands must have been a test of nature to endure my vision in spite of the distractions. I refused to swat the mosquitoes, only brushed them aside. The bloodsucker hordes swarmed over my hands, neck, and face, ready to be sacrificed in a noisy search of their stray vision, my blood. We were both determined, the mosquitoes and me. I refused to kill, to sacrifice another form of life for my vision. My stray vision had to be true and pure.

I must have fainted on the face of the rock from exhaustion and mosquito bites. I was awakened by the early morning sound of loons and the thin traces of the sunrise. My vision was stolen, and maybe for good reason, by the mosquitoes. Their search for a vision was much stronger than mine. I could not sacrifice a single life, and neither did the mosquitoes. They only sucked my blood overnight, and rejoiced in the morning over the remains of my body.

I paddled back to the dock. The woman who managed the canoe rental was shocked to see my swollen face and distorted hands. She shouted to her husband to help me into the house. They took care of me for three days, and during that wonderful time I told them about the seminar, and about my search for a stray vision without sacrifice. She was truly moved by my story, my trust of nature. Her husband was respectful of my story, but he seemed hesitant to show his emotions. He might have seen me as a stupid person. They invited me to live with them later in the summer, and to be their preacher on the boundary waters. You see, a stray vision changed my view of the world and without the sacrifice of life, not even the wicked mosquitoes. No, not really wicked, just hungry for my blood. Those mosquitoes might forever boast about my blood. I was invited to paddle around the boundary lakes as a preacher. I imagined that the mosquitoes would remember my name, my sacrifice, so that they might live.

Promissory was Anishinaabe. She promised not to be late, not to be a burden, not to be greedy, and yet she was compulsively early, never late, and was independent, not a strain to anyone, and she was very generous. She always promised in advance, for some reason, to cover the contingencies of time and situations. She sought the stories of stray visions in the ancient native rock images and paintings of the Great Lakes.

Promissory was intrigued by the native images of the great canoes of the early fur trade, the totemic depictions of animals and birds, hand prints, native healers, dancers, and hunters. She was especially curious about the humanoid figures that could be images of native tricksters or extraterrestrial aliens.

I am convinced that the alien other, or trickster from outer space, was either a stray vision imagined by native shamans and visionary artists, or the rock art images of the strange figures are actual portrayals of alien visitors to the granite Canadian Shield or Laurentian Plateau.

My heart travels with those native artists who created the images on granite. The artists imagined me, portrayed my presence in the future, and surely the mighty shamans envisioned the alien visitors. Some alien others might have become literary artists, and taunted the readers with strange metaphors of natural motion, the very images of motion that could recount the many light years of travel in space.

I wonder, were natives ever abducted by the alien others? Not plausible because the aliens had already been created by shamans. The shamans invented white men, but that was never any protection from slavery and dominance. Natives portrayed aliens as cosmic, visionary creatures, but the white men on stone were in boats and wore big hats. The fur traders were pictured in motion, and, like the aliens, the fur traders married into native families. Can you imagine how the federal government would react to the idea that there are native and extraterrestrial alien Métis? Actually there are probably alien others working in the Bureau of Indian Affairs. Do you suppose there are discrete alien pueblo cultures?

My union of chance with rock art images and aliens is a stray totemic vision, or maybe an ordinary trickster story or a rumor that has lasted for more than a thousand years. The most remarkable thing about these rumors and stray visions is that those who create stories of abduction describe the same sort of character. Carl Jung named the stories or alien objects as psychic products, and the stories about aliens are visionary rumors.

My stray vision of native rock artists and aliens is eccentric, but the simulations of aliens and natives are similar, rather obvious, and in that sense we share the same encounters as the other. Right, this is the time to declare that natives are not aliens, but the description of the other is similar. Natives are the aliens in captivity stories, but not tiny grays. My stories about the portrayal of others on rock art are stray visions. The images of little people, for instance, who vanish in the rocks and water, and the tiny alien grays are similar on the great face of the granite rocks.

General Badger was Anishinaabe. He wore a surplus military fatigue jacket with the insignia of a corporal and a patch of the First Cavalry Division. His hair was short with white patches, and his face was gray, pocked, and pointy. Altogether he was slouchy. Badger wore masks to the seminars, masks that he had constructed with papier-mâché, but the students totally ignored him because no one recognized the images. He was distant, smart, lazy, but not nasty. My cousin was surprised when two faculty poker players reported that General Badger had attended, in a mask, a recent concert by the Minnesota Orchestra.

My masks are actually famous composers of music. I thought that my best masks of George Frideric Handel and Ludwig van Beethoven would surprise the students in the seminar. I'm turned on by classical

music. My friends avoid music and the students avoid my masks.
How were they to know? Not by a mere mask and combat fatigues.
Badger is my name and that is my start of a stray vision. My
name is in the blank book, but nothing more, not even an idea about
a vision. I once expressed some interest in the junkyard, but never
pursued the subject in the seminar. Then in the last few weeks of the
seminar I decided to seek a vision on the prairie with my friend and
roommate. If you think I am weird you should meet him.

Dickie Mason wears military combat fatigues too and walks around
campus with the masks of military figures. We are the only masked
students on campus. Our masks are familiar, but we are invisible.
One day Dickie wore the mask of Lieutenant William Calley, the
guy who ordered the My Lai Massacre in Vietnam. Some people
were surprised when he was convicted of premeditated murder. No
surprise that the students shunned my roommate on campus. Dickie
expected to be shunned and continued to wear controversial masks
but for other reasons. He wanted to sense extreme experiences of
war, but only through a passive mask. Most students are not smart
enough to understand that idea. I never said much about his masks
and he never said much about my music. Sometimes my roommate
goes too far with the images. I convinced him not to wear a mask of
the Nazi war criminal Hermann Göring.

Dickie drove straight west and we stopped for burgers several times
along the way. We drove to the prairie but had no idea where to find
a stray vision. How do you search for nothing? The whole idea, if you
don't mind me saying so, seemed rather simple minded. You know,
writing about stray visions or anything in a blank book. Diaries are
not my style, and the seminar is weird, nothing like it on campus.
The whole thing, blank books, seminar stories, and street visions,
happens only because of you, Captain Shammer. Yes, you. Writing
in a blank book to you is something close to a stray vision. Well, not

really. Never met a teacher like you with so many stories. You make stories out of stories. Right, that's what the seminar is about.

So, we stopped at the first hill we found, a big hill, more like one of those mesa mounds on the prairie. We climbed up the mound, pitched a tent, smoked some dope, and waited for the glorious sun to set. The view from the mound was spectacular, and the sun crashed on the hazy horizon. That much right there, the nightly crash of the sun on the prairie was a stray vision, but not enough for the blank book. The colors of the sunset shot right past me, lighted our faces rosy, and then came the heavy darkness. Every night is heavy for me, too many bad memories of the dark. I never really sleep until the first scratch of light early in the morning. I have never written like this in a blank book.

I fell asleep in the tent the minute my head hit the earth. The dope is my escape from the dark, and it was very dark that night on the mound. Not a street light in twenty miles. Then, a few hours later, a bolt of lightning struck near the tent. I could feel the shock. My hair tingled. A sudden crack of thunder followed the blaze of light. We rushed out of the tent and watched bolts of lightning squirrel across the sky, an incredible sight that night. The lightning and thunder circled the mound, and then a gust of wind almost blew me down. I knew this was a very serious storm when leaves and trash flew past me on the wind. The wind and rain twisted around the mound, and the lightning blazed right nearby. I could feel the earth shudder from the thunder.

The lightning struck closer and closer so we linked our arms back-to-back and moved away from the last bolt, as if our moves would make a difference. We were about to be fried by lightning, so what else could we do. Dickie shouted at every blaze of light but his voice was choked back by the thunder. I never thought much about the time between a lightning bolt and thunder, but obviously we were *very close to being fried because the sound of the thunder cracked straightaway after the lightning.*

Dickie could not stop shouting at the lightning. We could not see enough in the dark to find our way down the mound, and it would have been even more dangerous. I couldn't think about the actual track of the lightning at the time, but it circled the mound. There was no safe way down the mound so we waited on the top to be fried alive. I thought it would be like instant death, sort of like the electric chair. Who has not tried to imagine the horrible experience of being electrocuted? Well, we were about to be shocked to death by a wild bolt of lightning. You might have read in my blank book about my execution by lightning over a stray vision on the prairie. Right, the blank book would be burned and leave only the charred remains of my stray vision.

The lightning pounded the mound, and the bolts struck closer and closer. My feet tingled from the streamers and jolts of electricity. Who could count the actual number of lightning strikes on the mound? How many? I don't know, maybe twenty, thirty, no, more than a hundred. I was knocked down several times by the force of the lightning and thunder. I was ready to give up, to roll over on my back and welcome electrocution. That would have been so easy to do, to give up, but like any person, and animals too, no one with a choice gives up in the face of death. No one. So, would you call that survivance? Right, survivance by stray visions.

The lightning storm on the mound was my stray vision. I write that now in the blank book. My stories about the experience have already changed from the first entry. You told me that about stories, and you taught me how to think about a stray vision instead of boredom and disaster, and my fear of the dark.

Trauma Queen was Yana from the Sacramento Valley in California. Her tribal affiliation could be one of many unreliable identity stories. She wore enough simulated native jewelry by neck, wrist, waist, and ears to establish a trade show colony.

Trauma was bright, blonde, curious, and seemed at first to be rather holistic about native victimry. So, she appeared to be more challenged by the sentiments of survivance than any other graduate student in the seminar. When Trauma touched her huge turquoise necklace and turned solemn about native cultures as aesthetic casualties the students turned away in silence, not a noticeable shun, but the gaze of absence. Shuns are communal and recoverable, but not the sense of absence. That gaze of absence started at the first session of the seminar when she announced that one of her famous ancestors was named Ishi by Alfred Kroeber.

Trauma was an uncertain pretender, and a generous advocate of panindian associations around the world. Many pretenders seem to congregate at international mea culpa associations. The native pretensions and absence of irony were much more bearable than the explanations of her bloodline and ancestry. Kinship with Ishi was over the top even for a pretender. She was earnest to a fault, and she was teaseable, but the students did not believe her native stories. The gaze of absence, however, vanished when she read and told stories about stray visions of survivance.

I have the creative power to imagine the coarse uniforms and dark closets at mission and federal boarding schools. My sorrow comes from the experiences of an imagined presence and abuse in the dormitories at the Carlisle Indian Industrial School, Wahpeton Indian School, The Bishop Hare School in South Dakota, and the Tuba City Boarding School on the Navajo Reservation in Arizona. I appreciate the anger and resentment of some boarding school students when they listen to me talk about my imagined agony. Why is there such resentment? No one owns the misery of experience, and yet every boarding school student has the absolute right of consciousness. Who does not know that much about misery? My imagination of these experiences is no less a burden, but not a right of actual testimony. My rights are emotional, the personal liberty to imagine stories about trauma, torture, and victimry.

Maybe the most intense resentment comes from those who create only one narrative of trauma, abasement, and humiliation, and that narrative is victimry. Why is victimry so convincing? Victimry is not native. Try to find that word, or the sentiment of the word victimry, in any native language. Yet, natives continue to live with the sentiments of victimry, not survivance. Why continue with the testimony of victimry? One reason is that the tragic world view and the sentiments of victimry makes better movies, but no native is better for the closure of memory as mere victimry. Where are the stories about native humor and irony? Most good citizens are convinced that natives have no sense of humor or capacity for irony. Can you imagine that historical absence? This is part of the great investment in the sentiments of victimry.

America is a mea culpa culture, a culture of pathos for tragedy, a culture that must create and maintain victims. So, many natives are encouraged by newspapers, churches, institutions, publishers, universities, corporations, and social workers to continue the stories of victimry. Where would anyone find native irony without tragedy, or better yet, the sentiments and stories of survivance?

Where?

Well, for a start, right here in my blank book of stray visions. Every native in the world should be given a blank book and required to oppose victimry with creative stories about survivance and stray visions. I imagine these situations of abuse and victimry. No one owns the rights of victimry because that sentiment should not exist and should be shunned in native narratives.

The victimry narrative is terminal, a political spectacle that serves publishers and big time moviemakers, not native experience and memory. The victimry spectacle does not heal students or anyone. Natives must create the sentiments and stories of survivance to honor the memory of traumatic experiences, and the narratives, of course, must be supported by documents and actual testimony.

Narratives of victimry are a cultural and psychological burden, and the causes of historical absence. No one can bear a sense of absence without resistance and irony. Stories of survivance and stray visions have the capacity to heal, to teach, reveal, resist, and to show native humor and irony. That idea is absolutely missing in narratives of victimry.

Captain Shammer is always elusive, and he refused to define the word survivance. The word is not in the dictionary. I wanted a definition of natural reason and survivance, some idea to compare, but that was exactly the point, he did not want us to compare one idea to another, like survivance to victimry. I understand that now, but there is always the temptation to derive meaning by comparison rather than by natural reason and experience. So, that does not give me a direct definition of survivance.

Yes, of course, there is no way to define a word that is actually in motion. I declare that postindians are in motion, a natural motion. Just like that, motion is a sense of presence and history is an absence. Now, the sentiment of natural motion and presence is survivance, and a stray vision of natural motion is survivance. I am closer to an appreciation and sense of the word, but there is always more motion to consider. How about theory, the very word that causes the nationalist to run for traditional cover? Say the words "theory" and "aesthetics" in the same sentence, and in any context, and the nationalists will consume the nearest traditions, a curious practice of cannibalism to save the past from theory.

Listen, language is theory. What else? Language is a mystery, and every word we mutter and write is a concept and theory. The words are never purified with a sacred lick of tradition. I know that much about the construction of concepts and the many turns and nuances of words. So now back to the sense and nuance of the word survivance.

Captain Shammer said that the theories of survivance are elusive. Right, about as elusive as a trickster. Maybe words were created by tricksters, or by shamans. My Captain said survivance was obscure and imprecise by definition. Now that makes sense to me. But he demands that we understand that survivance is true, invariably true, because the sentiments of survivance are found in stories about natural reason, motion, and stray visions.

The words seem to circle around to avoid comparison and definition. This is the time for me to run with the word and write at the end of my blank book that survivance is resistance, the resistance of stories, and survivance is the tease of nicknames, a communal and humane gesture, and vital irony, as vital as the irony dogs, and the moral courage to create a sense of presence and motion over absence and victimry. I like this sort of discourse about native motion and a sense of presence. My sense of presence must be in every word that leaves my mouth and lands in the book.

So, these are the last few words in my blank book of stray visions. I must create stories of survivance that renounce dominance and the unbearable sentiments of nationalism, tragedy, and victimry. My theories are humane and not the politics of traditions. Native traditions are inscrutable and there are no cultural representations of tradition. How could there be renditions in a native world of motion and survivance? Everything changes in a creative story. Only casino politics is a representation, or operatic traditions of victimry. Casino operas of native traditions are not comic or ironic, and certainly not stories of survivance.

My stories and stray visions are in the absolute motion of liberty. I am now more comfortable with natural reason, motion, and survivance, as you can read, but these words are the most elusive in my blank book.

Captain Shammer, this has been a truly memorable discovery of stray visions. I have a better understanding of irony. I have, you might say, become my own stray vision. I shall fight no, no, no more forever.

☞ 12 ☜

Earthdiver Auction

Captain Shammer posted the Department of Native American Indian Studies for sale—lock, stock, barrel, skin dunk, casino, and signature blank books—at a silent auction. Seventeen sealed tenders were received by the closing date of the auction. The bidders were present as the sealed tenders were opened and announced at a press conference in the department.

Dean Slash and Burn had encouraged the lucrative academic enterprises, and would never resist the actual sale of the department to the highest bidder. My cousin, the candidate with the least credentials, inspired students with stories of survivance, initiated the most eccentric and lucrative academic enterprises, and he outwitted the dean and faculty at every turn and birch bark edict.

Captain Shammer, the seventh and last native chairman of the department, was an elusive storier of survivance. The auction of the entire department, he declared, was the outcome of natural reason, a marvelous trickster scene about academic earthdivers.

The irony dogs and loyal houseboat mongrels were on stage in the law school auditorium and ready to bark at the auction tenders. Derrida nosed the natives on the aisles. Tear Catcher sat on a chair near the lectern and panted at the audience. Pontiac turned in circles and waved his enormous black tail at the students in the front row seats. Antipasto, the miniature descendant of Appetizer, paused, stared, and snuffled at the faculty seated on the aisles. Antipasto learned from her maritime mother never to bark in the presence of the dominant irony dogs. Lincoln, a recent irony dog graduate, walked down the aisle on his back legs and barked at every gesture of praise.

FIRST TENDER

The Short Hair Barber School of What Cheer, Iowa, tendered five hundred dollars cash and free haircuts for every native student in the department as long as the trees grow and the rivers flow. The natives in the audience at the press conference moaned and waved the barber tender out of the auction. Pontiac and Lincoln raised their heads and barked at the barber tender.

SECOND TENDER

The Magical Flight Genetic Engineers Limited promised new mutations of native futurity, and tendered one million dollars for the possession of the department and the absolute rights to portion and patent the postindian and fur trade genetic signatures combined in their laboratories. The audience turned savage and condemned the very scientific notions of postindian genetic mutations. Derrida ran in circles and barked at the genetic tender. Tear Catcher howled in the aisles. Antipasto snuffled, sneezed, and bounced on stage.

THIRD TENDER

The Native Sisters Bait, Wild Rice, and Tackle Shoppe of Calloway, Minnesota, tendered three thousand dollars to transmute the department into the most renowned feminist wild rice and angler academy in the world. The women at the press conference raised their fists and shouted their support of the fly and tackle shop tender. The women charged the seven male chairs and one dean for the trouble in the department. Captain Shammer announced that he would become a woman and handle the bait, but the women in the audience booed his tease. The tackle shop sisters proposed to bait the men and restore wild rice and mother earth. The mongrels barked at each other.

FOURTH TENDER

The Continental High Commission on Native Hesitation and Ambivalence of Fort Robinson, Nebraska, considered a tentative tender to change the actual name of the department to Undecided Studies. The High Commission proposed an arbitrary academic curriculum that would provide student credit for mere ambivalence. Dean Slash and Burn was hesitant about the tender, but the native students at the press conference praised the proposal of a new department that would grant course credit for indecision, absence, late attendance, reverie, and creative, ironic stories about final research papers consumed by mongrels. Some of the native students danced in the aisles and shouted their acceptance of the fourth tender without any other considerations. Lincoln and the other mongrels danced and barked in the aisles.

FIFTH TENDER

The Earthdivers, an association of native storiers, tendered the most direct and concise venture to reconsider and revise the entire academic practices of the university. The Earthdivers declared that higher education was creaky, overburdened with academic trivia, torrents of theory, crude ideologies, leisure nationalism, and farcical rituals in medieval gowns. Native tricksters and healers once created a new earth, a turtle island of survivance, and now all faculty, students, and deans must become academic earthdivers. The notion that history is a more significant narrative than native stories and literature must be overturned at the university. Traditional native storiers created the first historians to practice the sentiments of irony, but the monotheists, burdened by their wars and pretense of dominance, excluded the native sense of natural reason, totemic visions, and language play. Tear Catcher sneezed at the back of the auditorium, and the other irony dogs panted and smiled.

SIXTH TENDER

The Winnetou Indian Guides, a mundane and bogus native adventure of bourgeois fathers and sons, tendered one dollar and a promise to convert the department into a simulated warrior society. Indian Guides would encourage the students and faculty to decorate their faces with war paint, and wear plastic wing bones, stained chicken feathers, and beaded leather. The students shouted and mocked the proposal with obscene gestures and hokey hand signs. Winnetou was a fictional native warrior in the romantic novels by the German author Karl May. Indian Guides promised to raise money for an endowed chair in the name of Old Shatterhand, the narrator of the novels about the fictional Apache Winnetou. Derrida growled and barked on stage.

SEVENTH TENDER

The San Francisco Sun Dancers tender was concise and elusive, no tease, promise, money, or program. The Sun Dancers would only provided an urban vision of survivance by dance and ceremony. San Francisco, the mere city name, and native memories of the American Indian Movement occupation of Alcatraz were significant but the tender was not enough to rouse the audience. Antipasto and the other irony dogs were silent.

EIGHTH TENDER

The Native American Christians at the South Dakota State Penitentiary, assorted native felons sentenced to prison for larceny, car theft, and murder, presented the most unusual tender. The native inmates were not interested in the actual purchase of the Department of Native American Indian Studies. Rather, the converted inmates had invited the native students and faculty to auction their association in the penitentiary, the Native American Christians. The audience at the press conference embraced the tease of liberty. Derrida and Tear Catcher panted on stage.

NINTH TENDER

The National Association of Futurists tendered no specific price because the association was determined to acquire the department at any cost. The futurists explained that they never deigned to use the grammatical future tense. Consequently, they resisted the conditional sense, no *will* or future tender. The futurists declared by the actual purchase of the department a necessary presence of futurity at the university. The audience chanted *will, will, will* wannabes, and waved the futurists out of the auction. Derrida bounced, bayed, and barked at futurity. Pontiac howled at the tender.

TENTH TENDER

The General Custer Retirement Home in Roundup, Montana, tendered an ironic revision of the memorable Battle of the Little Big Horn. The Lakota and Northern Cheyenne warriors defeated George Armstrong Custer and the Seventh Cavalry on June 25, 1876. The retired military veterans proposed, a century later, that as the new senior proprietors of the department they would talk tough, demand military manners, basic combat training, salutes, and ceremonies, and restore the scare of war in native education with the stories of the Little Big Horn. The audience laughed and saluted the retired soldiers. Derrida rolled over and smiled. Antipasto rolled over twice, stretched his neck, and then covered his ears with his miniature paws.

ELEVENTH TENDER

Little Ramon, the past secretary of the department, was teased and promised the first option by the third and fifth chairmen to buy the department. The gesture of an option was ironic, nothing more, but he tendered two thousand dollars in cash, and more by credit if necessary. Ramon was certain that as the owner of the department he could easily complete his doctorate. He was implicated in the theft of books from the William Warren Memorial Library and resigned as secretary long before the arrival of the seventh chairman, Captain Shammer. The audience was silent. The irony dogs were once again silent.

TWELFTH TENDER

The Cambridge University Degrees of Cambridge, Minnesota, proposed to award advanced degrees to every native student in the department. The tender specified that the many creative, intelligent, brilliant, productive, elusive, and tricky people in the world should not be denied the highest academic degrees. Honorary doctorates would be awarded in Native American Consciousness and at least a dozen other fields of study. The students scorned the tender of advanced degrees because even the ironic practice of simulated academic certificates perpetuated the absurd notion of institutional knowledge. Derrida barked and howled at the tender.

THIRTEENTH TENDER

The most mysterious tender was from a wealthy widow who remained unnamed at the auction. She was concerned that great native ideas and cultural experiences might not be advanced at the university, and so she proposed to rescue and finance new programs in the department. The widow had inherited capital shares in several tobacco companies. Not even the native smokers were interested in the tobacco tender. Lincoln rolled over and sneezed.

FOURTEENTH TENDER

The Flat Earth Society of Fortuna, North Dakota, proposed to inaugurate a new course in the department, a course on how to walk over the edge of the earth with a complete sense of accomplishment. The Flat Earthers were determined to establish their peculiar terminal notions and practices at the university. Three native students mocked the tender by teetering on the edge of chairs. Derrida barked and howled at the very edge of the stage.

FIFTEENTH TENDER

The Whole Truth Health Institute of Santa Cruz, California, and Sedona, Arizona, proposed a singular diet that would save natives from the dubious tradition of fry bread, the ideologies of fast food, and the enticement of cultural nationalism. The Whole Truth tender was the only one that levied a fee for nutritional strategies, and provided for ceremonial native wakes and burials. The native students, no matter the health risks, would never accept any proposal that banished the tradition of fry bread. Derrida, Tear Catcher, and Pontiac barked at each other on stage.

SIXTEENTH TENDER

The Humphrey Resource Group, a corporation that promoted the acquisition and development of natural resources, timber, and minerals on reservations, tendered several million dollars in cash, options, and dividends to own the department. The Resource Group proposed to initiate special academic seminars on the management of natural resources on native reservations. The tender mentioned a furniture factory and military contracts on reservations as models of corporate resource and rescue development. The Resource Group borrowed the beloved name of the former senator and vice president, Hubert Humphrey. The mongrels growled in the aisles.

SEVENTEENTH TENDER

The Enticer Times, an association of seven newspapers in the United States, the United Kingdom, and France, tendered academic courses and practical experience in media communications. *The Enticer Times* proposed frequent and favorable media coverage of native ideas, publications, legal issues, and programs. The strategy of the tender, a media association proposal to acquire a native studies department, was not obvious at first. The last tender had enticed the audience, and the native students demanded more information about the media scheme. The senior editors of the international newspaper were aware that any news reports or feature stories about natives attracted readers around the world. The purchase of a native studies department would provide a constant source of native stories. The romantic notions of native absence and victimry were bankable sentiments at *The Enticer Times*.

Captain Shammer shouted and cursed the last tender and the name of the newspaper. *The Enticer Times* was no enticement at the auction of the department. Derrida barked at the tender of native misuse, absence, and victimry. The other irony dogs howled in the aisles.

The audience waited in anticipation for a decision on the seventeen tenders, but my cousin and the irony dogs had vanished in the excitement. Captain Shammer left behind his personal copy of *Stray Visions*, a deckle-edge blank book published by

Denivance Press. Only the single word "earthdivers" was printed on the first blank page.

Captain Shammer returned to the steady helm of the Red Lust, the family houseboat on Lake Itasca. The Earthdivers, an association of native storiers, won the auction and became the new owners of the Native American Indian Studies Department.

To order or obtain more information on these or other University of Nebraska Press titles, visit www.nebraskapress.unl.edu.